San Francisco
November 1999

SERMONS AND SODA-WATER

I

The Girl on the Baggage Truck

JOHN O'HARA

SERMONS AND SODA-WATER

I

The Girl on the Baggage Truck

RANDOM HOUSE • NEW YORK

Foreword to

SERMONS AND SODA-WATER

I am perfectly well aware that each of these three novellas could have been made into a full-length, 350-page-or-more, novel, and since the question is bound to come up, I shall try to answer it in advance: why did I choose the shorter form? The first, and probably the best, answer is that I wrote them this way because I wanted to. It is the answer that other authors will understand. However, I had reasons other than that. The form is one I like in spite of its unpopularity. Edith Wharton, Thomas Mann, Ernest Hemingway, Carl Van Vechten, David Garnett and James Hilton are among the few who have used the form successfully, but how few they are when you consider how many full-length novels are published in any one year, and the authors I have mentioned cover roughly fifty years. The resistance to the novella form comes from the non-professional public, the men and women who want their money's worth when they buy a book, and whose first test of a book is its avoirdupois. I don't quarrel with that right; the buyer of a book may set up any test or standard, or none at all. It is, of course, too bad that he must miss some good writing through the hefting test. I trust—but not too confidently—that a vast number of people will forget to weigh these small volumes.

I have another reason for publishing these stories in the novella form: I want to get it all down on paper while I can. I am now fifty-five years old and I have lived with as well as in the Twentieth Century from its earliest days. The United States in this Century is what I know, and it is my business to write about it to the best of my ability, with the sometimes special knowledge I have. The Twenties, the Thirties, and the Forties are already history, but I cannot be content to leave their story in the hands of the historians and the editors of picture books. I want to record the way people talked and thought and felt, and to do it with complete honesty and variety. I have done that in these three novellas, within, of course, the limits of my own observations. I have written these novellas from memory, with a minimum of research, which is one reason why the novella is the right form. I am working on a big novel that will take two years' research—reading, correspondence, travel—but it is my practice to be writing while I am doing research, and by the time I am ready to start writing the longer book, I may well have written two shorter ones. It will take me two years to *write* the longer book, and at fifty-five I have no right to waste time. Two years' research could mean a lot of wasted time while I wait for answers to letters and go on trips and yield to reading distractions that have nothing to do with the material I need for my longer, longest novel. That one *will* pass the hefting test, if it comes to pass.

I dedicate these books to my wife, Katharine Barnes O'Hara, and to my daughter, Wylie Delaney O'Hara, who sustain me.

JOHN O'HARA

Spring 1960
Princeton, New Jersey

The Girl on the Baggage Truck

When I was first starting out in New York I wrote quite a few obituaries of men who were presumably in good health, but who were no longer young. It was the custom on the paper where I worked that a reporter who had no other assignment was given this task, which most reporters found a chore but that I rather enjoyed. The assistant day city editor would tell you to prepare an obit on some reasonably prominent citizen, you would go to the office library and get out the folder of the citizen's clippings, and for the remainder of the afternoon you would read the clippings and appropriate reference books, and reconstruct a life from the available facts, keeping it down to forty lines or whatever length the subject's prominence had earned. It was good experience. One time I had to look up Jack Smedley, one of the richest oil men in the United States, and I discovered that his folder was so slim that you could have mailed it for the price of a two-cent stamp; while a Bronx politician of almost the same name had six bulging folders that cluttered up my desk. Later, when the two men died, the rich man was a Page One story all over the world, and the Bronx politician got thirty lines halfway down the column on the obituary page. You got what in more recent times was called a sense of values.

It was through an advance obituary assignment that I first learned that Thomas Rodney Hunterden was born in my home town. I had never known that, and my ignorance was certainly shared by most of my fellow townsmen. The baseball players, concert singers, vaudeville performers, Grade B Wall Street figures, clergymen, army officers, gangsters, and other minor celebrities who were natives or onetime residents of the town were always claimed with varying degrees of civic pride. The people in my home town not only remembered its former residents; they also clung to the memory of the famous visitors to the place—Theodore Roosevelt, John Philip Sousa, Colonel William F. Cody, Ruth St. Denis and Ted Shawn, Ignacy Paderewski, Harry Houdini, DeWolf Hopper, E. H. Sothern and Julia Marlowe, the

Borax 20-Mule Team, a stuffed whale on exhibition in a railway coach, the dirigible *Shenandoah,* two reigning Imperial Potentates of the Ancient Arabic Order of the Nobles of the Mystic Shrine, James J. Corbett, Arthur Guy Empey, Leopold Stokowski and the Philadelphia Orchestra, Paul Whiteman and His Orchestra, Billy Sunday, Dr. Frank Buchman, Dr. Russell H. Conwell, and William Jennings Bryan, to name a few who had passed through or over the town. The people of my town were as quick with reminiscences of a suffragan bishop who lived in New England as they were with stories about a whoremaster who operated in Atlantic City, and it just was not in character for them to forget Thomas Rodney Hunterden.

The next time I was home on vacation I had a beer with an old-time newspaper man who knew everything about everybody. "Claude, did you ever hear of Thomas R. Hunterden?" I asked.

"Thomas Rodney Hunterden, d, *e,* n? Sure. Why?"

"Did you ever know him?"

"How would I know *him?*"

"Because he was born in Gibbsville, and he's about your age."

Claude shook his head. "He wasn't born in Gibbsville. I'd know it if he was," said Claude quietly.

"I could take some money away from you on that," I said.

"I'll bet you a new hat."

"No, no bet. I *know*."

It was afternoon, and the public library was open till nine in the evening, so we had a few more beers and then went to look up Thomas R. Hunterden in *Who's Who in America*. My friend Claude Emerson, who was half Pilgrim stock and half Pennsylvania Dutch, was so miserable at being caught in an error that we went back to the speakeasy and drank more beer, but he was not so talkative. Several weeks after I returned to New York a note came from Claude.

Dear Jim:

If Thomas R. Hunterden claims to have been born in Gibbsville, the man is a liar. I spent an entire day at the Court House in among the birth and tax records. No one named Hunterden was ever born in Lantenengo County since records have been kept, nor has anyone paid taxes under that name. You have aroused my curiosity. Wish I could track this down. If you get the opportunity to interview Hunterden, would be much obliged to hear what you learn.

> Yours sincerely,
> Claude Emerson

The opportunity to interview Thomas R. Hunterden was a long time coming. I was fired from the paper and it was several months before I got a job as a press agent for a movie company. My interest in Hunterden was non-existent until one morning when I was at Grand Central Terminal, meeting the Twentieth Century Limited. Charlotte Sears, who was one of my employer's not-quite-top stars, was coming in on the Century, and I was there to handle the reporters and photographers. There were three photographers and a reporter from the *Morning Telegraph,* and we were a little group down on the platform, conspicuous only because the photographers had their cameras out and camera cases hanging from their shoulders. The fellow from the New York Central press department came to me with the information that the car in which Charlotte had a drawing-room would be at a point farther up the platform, and our group accordingly moved on.

I noticed casually that a tall gentleman in a Chesterfield and carrying a silver-mounted walking stick was standing at approximately the point toward which we were headed. He paid no attention to our group until he saw the cameras, then there was no mistaking his reaction for anything but panic. He saw the cameras, he put a yellow-gloved hand to his face, and he quickly walked—almost ran—past us and up the ramp and out of sight. I vaguely recognized him as a man whose photographs I had seen but whom I had not seen in person. In a minute or two the Century pulled in and I had other things to think about than a man who did not want his picture taken. I had my job to do.

I reintroduced myself to Charlotte Sears, whom I had met on previous occasions, and we posed her sitting on a baggage truck with her legs crossed and an inch or two of silk-stockinged thigh showing. The little man from the *Telegraph* asked her the usual questions about the purpose of her visit, the future of talking pictures, the rumored romance with an actor who everyone in the industry knew was a drug addict and a homosexual, and the chance of her doing a stage play. The photographers and reporter finished their jobs and Chottie Sears and I were alone. "I have a limousine to take you to the hotel," I said.

"I think I'm being met," she said.

"I'm afraid not," I said, guessing. "I think the photographers frightened him away."

"Mr. Hunterden? Oh, Lord, of course," she said. "But he *was* here?" I immediately identified Hunterden as the man with the cane.

"Yes, he was here," I said. "But as soon as he saw those cameras . . ."

"Of course. I should have warned him. All right, Jim, will you take me to the hotel? Have you had your breakfast?"

"I had a cup of coffee," I said.

"That's all I've had. Have breakfast with me."

On our way to the hotel I told her about the interviews we had scheduled for her and the public appearances she was expected to make. "I hope you haven't booked me for any evening engagements," she said. "If you have, that's your hard luck."

"A charity ball," I said. "At the Astor."

She shook her head. "Nothing in the evening. Tell Joe Finston I have other plans."

"*You* tell him."

"All right, I'll tell him. And believe me, when Finston knows who the plans are with, he won't raise any objections. Well, *you* know. You saw him at the station. To think how close he came to getting his picture in the papers. That was a narrow escape. I should have warned him. Do you know him, I mean personally?"

"No, I've never met him."

"He hates reporters and those people. He has a positive aversion to them. Are you married, Jim?"

"No."

"I know you weren't the last time I was here, but things happen fast in this life. Why I asked is, while I'm in town will you do the honors? Take me out and so forth?"

"That's no hardship, and it's what I'm paid for anyway."

"The only trouble is, you'll have to sort of stand by. I won't know when I'll need you."

"I could guess that," I said.

She took a bath while breakfast was on the way to her suite and I was disposing of the telephone calls from high school interviewers, jewelry salesmen and furriers. "No call from that certain party?" she said.

"Not unless he was pretending to be from New Utrecht High," I said. "Or maybe he was the man just in from Amsterdam. I don't know his voice."

"You don't have to know his voice," she said. "The manner gives him away. He's used to giving orders."

"So I'd infer, although I have nothing to do with the stock market. Eat your breakfast. It's a cold and wintry day."

"I wish he'd call, damn it."

"He will. Have some coffee."

"What do you know about his wife?"

"Mrs. Thomas Rodney Hunterden, a name on the society pages. A doer of good works, I gather. That's all. I could look her up if you want me to."

"No, I just thought you might have some information offhand."

"I don't get around in those circles," I said.

"You and me both," said Chottie. "The way I was brought up, anybody that finished high school is in society."

"Oh, come on," I said.

"Really," she said. "I can do simple arithmetic and I read a lot, but that's the extent of my culture. And travel. It's a good thing I liked to travel or I'd have been bored to death by the time I was twelve. But I liked it. Split weeks in Shamokin and Gibbsville, P A."

"Be careful. That's where I come from."

"Shamokin?" she said. "The Majestic Theatre."

"No, Gibbsville."

"The Globe. I played the Globe in vaudeville, twice, and I did a split week in Gibbsville with a road company of *The Last of Mrs. Cheyney*. You didn't happen to catch me in that, did you?"

"I'd left there by then," I said. I do not know why I refrained from mentioning Gibbsville as the birthplace of her Mr. Hunterden. I think it was because she was upset about the photographers at Grand Central and nervous about the telephone call that had not yet come.

"I was young for the part," she said. "But I was glad to get the job. I had to get out of New York. I don't mean I had to because I was forced to or anything like that, but there was a young polo player in love with me. A strong infatuation, call it. He was a nice kid, but a kid. His parents made life very difficult for me."

"Threatened you?"

"Anything but. They belonged to the school that thinks a young man ought to sow his wild oats, and I was his wild oats. Tame wild oats. I didn't have a bad reputation, and they sort of approved of me as Junior's girl friend, just as long as I didn't show any signs of wanting to marry him. Oh, I visited them and I went for a cruise on their yacht. But then I began to ask myself, what was I? What was I getting out of it? I was a combination of nursemaid and mistress. It was a dandy arrangement—for them and for Junior. Then I began to get sore. I hate being a chump. Other girls I knew would have taken him for plenty. They figured I was just too nice to be that kind of a girl. So I got out of New York."

"But why? There's something missing here."

"Because I was beginning to get a little stuck on the kid and there was no future in it. I wasn't in love with him, but he had charm and I wasn't going out with anyone else, so I began to get stuck on him. But two weeks on the road and he was nothing to me, nothing." She had a sip of coffee. "When I'm on the road I'm a great sightseer. I go for walks. Other people on the bill, or in the company, they travel all over the country, thousands of miles, and all they ever see is the inside of one theatre after another. All they ever read is *Billboard* and *Zit's*. Maybe the *Racing Form* and the *Christian Science Monitor*. But they never read the local papers, or books or magazines. Some of them don't even bother to read their notices, because half the time the hick critics are on the take from the local theatre manager. Those that aren't, they pan everything. We got one notice on *Mrs. Cheyney* that didn't even know Freddie Lonsdale was an Englishman. What a business!" The telephone rang. It was Joe Finston, welcoming the star to New York and inquiring whether she was being well taken care of.

She hung up. "Joe Finston. That heel. Last year he'd have been here in person, but the grosses are down on my last two pictures, so he uses the telephone. This call was to soften me up. He'll be nice to me because he wants to talk me out of my contract, but fat chance he has. I have three more years to go, raises every year automatically. The only way I'll let him out of the contract is if he pays me one hundred per cent of what the contract calls for."

"You know what he'll do, don't you?"

"Sure. Put me in one stinker after another till I holler for help. But it won't work with me. I'll be on the set and made up at six o'clock every morning. I'll go on location to Patagonia. I know all the tricks. Stills that make me look fifty years old. But I worked a lot harder for sixty dollars a week than I do now for six thousand. Finston doesn't know that. Finston isn't show business. He's a picture-business nephew. He doesn't realize that it would be cheaper to settle the contract for a hundred per cent on the dollar now than put me in four or five stinkers."

"Would you settle now?"

"Did he tell you to ask me that?"

"No."

"Then I'll tell you, yes. I'd settle now, this minute. Do you know how much I have coming to me on the contract? Only $1,488,000. That's forty weeks left of this year, and three more years with raises. If you figure interest, that's over a million and a half. I won't get it. He won't settle. But he'd be much smarter if he did, because if you put a star in a stinker you have a bigger stinker than if you had no star."

"You said it. Would you quit the movies if you got all that money at once?"

"Nobody ever quits the movies, Jim. They go into enforced retirement. The talkies killed off those that couldn't read lines or had voices that wouldn't record.

But they didn't quit. A queen doesn't—what's the word?"

"Abdicate?"

"Abdicate. And that's the way you're treated while you're a star. Like a queen. Bring in those grosses, and you're treated like royalty. Begin to slip a little, and choose the nearest exit. But that isn't abdicating. That's escaping from the angry mob. I'll do what others have done. I'll take the money and come back here and wait for a good play. The difference is, if you have a flop on Broadway, it doesn't count against you the next time out. And if I happen to get a hit on Broadway, the next time I go to Hollywood I'll start at ten thousand! And maybe Joe Finston will be the one who pays it. Wouldn't that be nice?"

"It sure would." I got up and looked at the scrambled eggs that were being kept warm over an alcohol burner. "You sure you won't have some solid food?"

"All right," she said.

I started to dish out the eggs and the telephone rang. "You want me to go in the other room?" I asked.

"I'll go."

We both guessed it was Hunterden, and we were right. She went to the bedroom and was gone about fifteen minutes. When she came back she was calm and self-possessed. Whatever had been said on the telephone, her composure was now that of a star. I dished out the eggs again and she ate a big breakfast, speaking very little. "I was hungry," she said. "I want to go to the theatre every night I'm in town. Will you arrange for the tickets? I may not *get* there every night, but when I can't, you take some friend of yours. Here." She handed me a $100 bill.

"What's this for? I'll get the tickets from a scalper and have them put on your hotel bill."

"Your expenses."

"I put in an expense account at the office."

"I'm trying to give you a little present, you idiot," she said.

"Oh. Well, thanks. I can use it. Thanks very much."

"I should thank you. You got me through a difficult two hours. Imagine what I'd have been like, missing him at the station and then sitting here fidgeting."

"You go for this guy in a great big way, don't you?"

"I guess I do. Why else would I give a darn? Why else would I keep all my evenings free?"

All this was thirty years ago, as remote-seeming to many people today as the Gay Nineties had seemed to me. New York now is as different from New York then as New York then was from London. The one pervasive factor in all our lives was Prohibition, which made law-breakers of us all and gave a subtly conspiratorial, arcane touch to the simple act of dining out. Even that was phony, for there were only a few speakeasies which you could not talk your way into, where you had to be known. Indeed, it is harder to get a table at the best restaurants today than it was to gain admittance to the illegal cafés of those days. The other pervading factor, whose influence has been exaggerated in retrospect, was the national greed, the easy dollar in the stock market. But Prohibition, with the speakeasy, and the stock market, with the lucky dollar, facilitated romances like that between Charlotte Sears and Thomas R. Hunterden. Men like Hunterden have always had mistresses like Chottie Sears, but the speakeasy made it all so much simpler and the stock market paid the bills.

In the beginning I mentioned an oil millionaire whose newspaper clippings failed to fill a single folder. That was not true of Thomas R. Hunterden. His record filled three or four folders, and when I visited the library of the newspaper from which I had been fired, and checked what I had read, I now noticed that not a single clipping was dated prior to 1917. According to the other information available, Hunterden was in his early forties when the United States entered the war. His age had kept him out of the army draft, but there was no mention of any war activity whatever, either in his clippings or in the standard reference books of the period. In his brief *Who's Who* sketch he stated that he was born in Gibbsville, Pa., on April 2, 1876, and educated in "public schools" but did not say where; and there was no mention of his parents, a most unusual oversight if it was an oversight. The next item stated that he married Alice Longstreet in 1919. If there were any children they were not mentioned. After that followed a list of corporations of which he was board chairman: American Industrial Corporation, British-American Transportation, Throhu Petroleum, Omega Development, and Omega Holding. He then listed his clubs: the New York Yacht, the Bankers, and several golf and yacht clubs in Florida and South America. The only address he gave was his office on Lower Broadway. The Social Register provided one additional bit of information: Alice Longstreet was not her maiden name. She had been married to a man named Longstreet and her maiden name was Alice Boyd.

I then looked up all the Longstreet clippings and I found what I wanted. In 1918 Forrest Longstreet committed suicide by jumping from a window in his office in the financial district. Surviving were his wife, the former Alice Boyd, and two daughters. Longstreet had been quite a fellow. In the clippings he was often described as the sportsman-financier, prominent clubman, big-game hunter, aeronaut, foxhunter, and so on. He had played football at Harvard and had once set a record for driving his racing car from Rome to Paris. The newspaper photographs of him showed a handsome man with thick black hair and eyebrows, a black moustache, and white even teeth. The pictures confirmed my guess that he had been a wild man. It was not a particularly shrewd guess; the clippings gave the clues.

Sporting accidents, expeditions into Africa, a suit for breach of promise, a swimming race from the Battery to Bedloe's Island. I was too young and too deep in the Pennsylvania mountains to have heard of Longstreet, but now he interested me as much as Hunterden, and I knew that in finding out about the one I would be learning about the other.

I had a speakeasy friend named Charley Ellis, who was my age and who was my principal connection with New York society, as I was his with the Broadway-theatre-newspaper world. Charley had a job that he did not take very seriously, and he was easily persuaded to have me to lunch at his club.

"Why the sudden interest in old Forrest Longstreet?" he asked, when I began to question him. "Not that he was so very old. I guess he'd be about fifty-five or -six if he'd lived. He was a friend of my old man's."

"Did you know him yourself?"

"Oh, sure. He used to take me for rides in his car. He had a car called a Blitzen-Benz. We'd go like hell out the Vanderbilt Parkway and on the way back he'd give me cigarettes. Now that I think of it, I guess he was my godfather. Yes, he was."

"Why did he do the dry dive?"

"What's this for? You're not going to put it in the paper, are you?"

"What paper? I don't work for a paper any more."

"No, but you might again. This has to be under the hat."

"It will be."

"Well, Forrie Longstreet was mixed up in some very suspicious stock promotion, and when he killed himself his family gave out the story that he did it for the insurance. The insurance was supposed to pay back his friends that went in on the stock deal. Actually, they were paid back by other members of his family. He blew all his own money, but the Longstreets still had plenty and they came through. My old man collected something, I know."

"What about his wife?"

"What about her?"

"Well, how did he leave her fixed?"

"Oh. Well, it didn't really matter, I guess. She married a fellow called Hunterden, supposed to be in the chips."

"Which one don't you like? Hunterden, or Longstreet's widow? You're holding out on me."

"I know I am, Jim. I don't know what you want this information for, and I liked Forrie Longstreet. Let him rest in peace."

"I think Hunterden is a phony. I know he is, in some things, and I want to find out how much of a phony. I have no intention of writing an exposé, or giving it to the papers, but I've had my curiosity aroused. He's having an affair with Charlotte Sears, and I like her. It's none of my business. She's a big girl now and not a great friend of mine, but she's on the up-and-up. I did a little digging on Hunterden and I happened to come across Longstreet's name."

"Charlotte Sears is much too good for him, but as you say, if she's having an affair with him, what business of ours is it to interfere?"

"Not interfere, but be ready when the roof caves in. She trusts me, and she's a good egg. Would you like to meet her? I'm taking her to the theatre tonight. Meet us at Tony's, twelve o'clock."

"I've met her. She was going around with Junior Williamson a couple of years ago. Not that she'd remember me, but I'd like to see her again."

We said no more about Forrest Longstreet or Thomas Hunterden. Late that night Charlotte Sears and I went to Tony's, a speakeasy that was a meeting place for theatrical and literary people, and Charley Ellis joined us. He was too polite to remind her that they had met in the past, but she remembered him and he was pleased. "What's Junior up to these days?" she asked.

"Oh, he's talking about going into politics."

"Is that his idea, or his wife's?"

"His, I guess. He doesn't know what to do with himself."

"I guess when you have as much money as he has, it gets to be a problem. You don't feel like making any more money, and if you're in love with your wife, you don't go on the make. At least not yet. But he will. There isn't much there, you know. This may sound like sour grapes, but Junior's a mama's boy."

"That's no secret," said Charley Ellis.

"Maybe not, but it's the secret of his charm."

"How could it be?"

"A man wouldn't understand that, Mr. Ellis. As soon as a girl discovers that Junior's a mama's boy, every girl thinks she's going to be the real mama."

"A strange way to look at it."

"You're talking to somebody that learned it through experience. Oh, well, he was a nice kid and I guess he always will be. The women will vote for him. Once. What's he going to run for? Governor?"

"He hasn't said, but I doubt if he'd run for governor."

She laughed. "I could defeat him."

"You'd run against him?"

"Hell, no. I'd support him. The minute I opened my mouth the Democrats would thank me for saving them the trouble. Can you imagine the horror at Republican headquarters if I came out for Junior?"

"You should have been a politician," said Charley.

"Should have been? I am, every day of my life. Ask Jim. In our business Al Smith wouldn't last a minute. By the way, Jim, Joe Finston is taking me to lunch tomorrow, apropos of nothing at all."

Two acting couples invited themselves to our table and in a little while we all went to the Central Park Casino. Before saying goodnight Charley Ellis asked me to meet him for lunch the next day, and I said I would be glad to.

"That was fun last night," said Charley Ellis, at lunch.

"Yes, we didn't get home till after seven. We went to Harlem."

"I have to go through the motions of holding down my job," he said. "She's a good egg, Charlotte Sears. Confusing, though. I kept thinking she was still carrying the torch for Junior Williamson."

"Maybe she is."

"She's wasting her time. I didn't want to say anything, but Junior has his next wife all picked out already. Sears is right. There isn't much there. I like Sears."

"Yes, I can tell you do. Why don't you grab her away from Hunterden?"

"Somebody ought to. Hunterden is bad business."

"Take her away from him. She liked you. She said so."

He smiled. "She said so to me while I was dancing with her. As a matter of fact, Jim, and very much *entre nous*, I'm seeing her tonight."

"Good work," I said. "Fast work, too."

"Well, I thought it was worth a try. Maybe she just wants to talk about Junior, but we'll get on other subjects."

"I'm sure you will. I wonder what she plans to tell Hunterden," I said. "You know, I never got the feeling that she was in love with Hunterden as much as she was afraid of him."

"He's bad business. And you want to hear about Forrie Longstreet. He didn't kill himself over money."

"You more or less implied there was another reason."

"It was his wife. Forrie was a wild man. Cars and air-planes and all that. But he was crazy about Aunt Alice. We weren't related, but when I was a kid I called her Aunt Alice. Absolutely devoted to her, Forrie was. And apparently she was in love with him till this Hunterden guy came along. Hunterden went to Forrie with a busi-ness proposition that looked like easy money, just for the use of Forrie's name, and that's how Hunterden met Alice. Forrie lost his dough, his good name, and his wife, all to the same guy. My old man told me Alice didn't even wait six months before she married Hunter-den. But I guess she's paying for it."

"How so?"

"Everybody dropped her like a hotcake. My mother wouldn't have her in the house, even before she married Hunterden. My mother of course was one of those that knew what was going on between Alice and Hunterden, and I gather she had a talk with her, but Alice wouldn't listen. You think you come from a small town, but what you may not realize is that there's a very small town right here in New York, composed of people like my mother and father. They never see anyone outside their own group and have no desire to, and believe me, the gate was closed on Alice Longstreet. The portcullis is lowered and the bridge over the moat has been raised, permanently."

"I see her name in the paper all the time."

"Yes, and you should hear my mother on the subject.

'Alice still doing public penance, I see.' That's what Mother says about Alice and her charities."

"How do the boys downtown feel about Hunterden?"

"Depends on what boys you're talking about. My old man and his friends give him the cut direct, and any time they hear he's in anything, they stay out of it."

"How did he get in all those clubs?"

"There's a funny thing about clubs. If the right people put you up, a lot of members hesitate to blackball you. The members figure that a man's sponsors must have their own good reasons for putting him up, and the members are inclined to respect those reasons, even in a case like Hunterden's. And there are some clubs he'll never get in."

"This one, for instance?"

"Oh, hell, this isn't what it used to be. I mean it isn't as hard to get in. There was a time when all the members knew each other. Now as I look around I don't even know all the guys my own age. This is where Forrie Longstreet used to hang out. I'll take you upstairs and show you some pictures of him."

"I've seen some. He was a dashing figure."

"In everything he did. He belonged in another age, when all gentlemen carried swords."

"I don't know, Charley. In Walpole's time fellows like Longstreet got into debt and had to do business with guys like Hunterden."

"So they did, but the Hunterdens never met the Longstreets' wives."

"I wonder."

"Well, maybe they did," said Charley Ellis. "You *like* to think things were better long ago."

"Better for whom?" I said. "Two hundred years ago I wouldn't be sitting here with you."

"If you say that, you know more about your family two hundred years ago than I do about mine. I'm not an ancestry snob, Jim. Maybe you are, but I'm not. My objection to Hunterden isn't based on who his grandfather was. Neither was my father's or mother's. It's what Hunterden himself was. And is. I consider Charlotte Sears more of a lady for dropping Junior Williamson than I do Alice Longstreet for marrying Hunterden. When I was in prep school I remember seeing pictures of Charlotte Sears, before she had a reputation as a movie actress. Around the same time Alice, Aunt Alice Longstreet, was a beautiful lady who was a friend of my mother's. But now Charlotte Sears is the beautiful lady, and Alice Hunterden is a social climber, trying to climb back. And having hard going."

"Very instructive conversation," I said. "And that isn't sarcasm."

"A little sarcasm. You know, Jim, people from your side of town, they choose to think that all the snobbery is concentrated in people like my mother and father. But all my father and mother want to do is see their friends and mind their own business. That's the way they like to live, and since they can afford it, that's the way they do live. And incidentally, money has very little to do with it. I know damn well my old man has friends that don't make as much money as you do. But they *are* his *friends*. Whereas, on Broadway, and the Hollywood people, a big star doesn't want to be seen with anyone that isn't just as big a star or a little bigger. And among those people there's nothing worse than a has-been. With my father and mother there is no such thing as a has-been." He smiled to himself.

"What?" I said.

"I said to the old man this morning that I'd been out with Charlotte Sears last night. 'Tell me about her,' he said. 'What's she like?' He's never met her, but he's seen her movies and plays, and he was really interested. But he doesn't want to know her any better, and neither would my mother. That isn't snobbishness, but you might think it is, and I guess Charlotte would too. You're the snob of us two."

"Why do you say that? It may be true," I said.

"One night when you took me to that place called Dave's Blue Room."

"I remember," I said.

"We sat down at a table, a booth, and you knew everybody there. They all said hello to you and they gave me the cold stare till you introduced me. 'Charley Ellis, of the *Daily News*.' Then they relaxed."

"Why was I a snob? Maybe they were, but why was I?"

"Because you were embarrassed in your own crowd, to be seen with somebody that wasn't a member of the crowd. You had to explain who I was. If you hadn't been a snob, you'd have just introduced me as Charley Ellis, or even Charley Ellis, customer's man at Willetts & Ellis."

"You're right," I said.

"Well, Charley Ellis, customer's man, has to make a few phone calls, but if you'd like to hang around for a while I'll play you some pool."

"Thanks, but I'm going up to see La Sears. She has a fan-magazine interview at four o'clock. Any message for her?"

"Just that I'm looking forward to seeing her tonight."

Chottie's maid let me in and I had a half-hour wait before Chottie turned up. It was immediately apparent that her luncheon with Joe Finston had not gone well. "Do you know a good cheap gangster that's looking for a night's work?" she said.

"I know several. Your candidate's Finston?"

"Who else? He offered me a picture that's been turned down by everybody on the lot, and of course when I said no, he said he was going to offer it to me by registered letter, and then if I turned it down he'd put me on suspension."

"That's what you pay an agent for."

"I know, but my agent is on the Coast and this little maneuver is all Finston's, in New York. Oh, I'll figure out something, but this heel, this nephew, Finston, he's doing all he can to spoil my visit. He wants to get out of the contract and then show his uncles what a smart boy he is. To show you how cheap he is, he said if he wanted to, he could legally notify me in New York, today, and if I refused to do the picture, I'd not only go on suspension. I'd even have to pay all my expenses while I'm here."

"Well, from what I know of him, he'd do it."

"Jim, you stay out of it. I know you're on my side, but I don't want you to lose your job on account of me."

"Finston won't fire me, not right away. He wants to get some personal publicity in the New York papers and he's convinced I'm the one that can get it for him. Chottie, I haven't been with the company very long, and you have, but I know something you may not know."

"What's that?"

"Finston has his eye on the Coast. He'd do anything to get in the production end. But his uncles don't want any part of him out there. They don't even like it when he takes trips out there. Don't forget, it's his mother that's a Rosenbaum, not his father. The Rosenbaum brothers want to keep Joe Finston here in the home office, as far away from production as he can get."

"I knew some of this, but not all. I didn't know he was trying to get into production."

"Oh, yes. When he was in college he wanted to be a writer. He told me that himself. He wants to fire all the writers on the Coast and get all new ones. Also directors. He thinks he knows about directing."

"He couldn't direct a blind man across the street."

"I'm sure of it. Well, if I were you, I'd stall him till you go back. Let him say or do anything he pleases. Then when you get back to the Coast, go see Morris Rosenbaum and tell him you understand Finston is getting ready to take over production. If he recovers from his stroke, you tell him you heard a lot of rumors to that effect while you were here. In fact, you say to Morris you got that impression because Finston wanted you to star in this turkey and tried to talk you into it all the time you were in New York."

"I think I'll marry you, Jim."

"Just the way I am? I ought to go out and buy a few things. And you have a date tonight with a friend of mine."

"Well, he asked me. And you didn't."

"I didn't, because it's my job to take you out, and I do it on company money. I don't mean anything to you, Chottie, so don't pretend I do."

"Truthfully, you never did before, but this trip—I don't know. I never knew you before. I'll break the date with Ellis?"

"Oh, no. You keep the date with Ellis."

"Will you meet us later?"

"No."

"Well then, don't be jealous of Ellis. Jealous of Ellis! Well listen to the girl."

I decided to catch her off balance. "Where is Hunterden?"

"Hunterden? Why?"

"Okay, it's none of my business."

"No, it isn't," she said haughtily, so haughtily that I guessed something had gone wrong.

"Sorry I mentioned it," I said. "Now about this dame that's coming to interview you. She's new, but watch her. She's meek and mild, and asks innocuous questions, but she's out to make a score and we've had a little trouble with her. She doesn't write the usual fan-magazine slop."

"Everybody's out to make a score, in one way or another. I wish I had six children and lived in Chillicothe. Any Chillicothe, just so it wasn't New York or Hollywood."

"You've seen all those towns, but you never lived in them, and you never could."

"Don't be hard on me, Jim. I don't know where I'm at. If you want to know the truth, I'm scared."

"Of what?"

"Hunterden. Ellis. Finston. Junior Williamson. Oh, *he* phoned. He saw in the paper I was in town, and he quote just called up to chat unquote. So don't you add to my troubles, please. On the train East I had everything all worked out so neatly. Hunterden would meet me and we'd see each other and maybe get a few things settled. But he ran away from the photographers. And then I met your friend Ellis and I liked him, but he's on the make. Not that I blame him, but here I go with Junior again, only this time his name is Ellis. And I'm scared of Finston. He has a mean little face and I don't think it's going to be easy to fight him." She stopped. "I'm ashamed of myself, Jim. I tried flirting with him, but he wasn't having any. Ashamed and scared. An ugly little man like that ought to be easy to handle, but he just looked at me like I was another man. No, not like another man. He wouldn't have the guts to look at another man with such contempt. Do you know what he said? I can hardly repeat it."

"Don't if you don't want to."

"There we were in the middle of Sardi's and I was trying to use my feminine wiles, hating it but acting. And he said, 'Any time you want to put your clothes back on, let's talk contract.'"

"Did you have any answer to that?"

"Yes, I said I hoped he got a good look because the only way he ever would would be in his imagination. That's when I wished I could mention Hunterden's name, but how can I? I haven't seen Hunterden since I've been in New York. If you were a woman you'd know what I'm going through with Finston and Hunterden. Slapped in my famous teeth by a little horror I wouldn't even step on, and given the absent treatment by a big shot. And what's in between? An ex-college boy on the make, your friend Ellis. Don't be hard on me, Jim. I'm scared."

"I'll get you out of this interview."

"Can you? I couldn't face a tough dame this afternoon."

"You go downstairs and wait in the limousine. I'll wait till she gets here and tell her you're launching a battleship, or something. I'll get rid of her. I suggest you go for a drive through the Park and come back in about an hour."

"I don't want to be alone," she said. "Please, Jim. You get rid of her and then come down and go for a drive with me."

"Well then, park the car up Fifth Avenue and I'll join you as soon as I can."

I was not in love with Chottie and I never could be. She was a public person and I had already observed that a public person could only be in love with another public person; in Chottie's case another star, a famous young heir, a mysterious but nonetheless public figure like Hunterden. And yet as I made my way to the limousine, and as we drove through the Park and over to Riverside Drive, I wanted to protect her, to keep her from injury, to shield her from roughness. In the Park she reached over and took my hand.

"What are you thinking about, Jim?"

"You."

"I thought so," she said. She did not go on, and neither did I. If I told her that I wanted to protect her, I would be taking away her strongest protection, which was her belief in her own toughness. I saw her clearly as something gay and fragile that could be hurt and even destroyed, but she was as proud of her independent spirit as she was of her beauty and talent. I let her think whatever she was thinking, and for the remainder of the ride she encouraged me to talk about myself and jobs I had had. Back at the hotel entrance she said, before getting out of the car: "Do you want to keep the car?"

"You mean, don't come up," I said.

"That's what I mean. Don't come up. This would be a very bad time to start anything, if we ever are."

"And if we don't now, we probably never will," I said.

"Probably," she said. "I'll give you a wonderful kiss and you'll always know we could have."

"If you give me a wonderful kiss, we will," I said.

"Yes, I guess so. Then no kiss, but when you get old and think back on your girls, I give you permission to include me. We just as good as. Thank you, Jim."

She left me, and I found that the factual part of my mind was busy wondering how old she was. Until that moment she had been among those actresses whose beauty and fame, while they last, make them impervious to questions as to their real names and real ages. But we had come very close to making love, and she herself had been the one to mention age. It was on her mind, and now it was on mine. Until then I would have accepted any age under thirty as a true one for her. With some sense of treacherous guilt I told the driver to take me to my newspaper alma mater, and I passed the next two hours in the files.

Allowing for margins of error, I found that she was no less than thirty-five, and quite possibly thirty-eight. Shows and plays she had been in, the kinds of roles she had played, established her age within those three years. My first thought when I considered her age was that at the time that I was begging my father to buy me an air rifle, Charlotte Sears had her name in lights in Herald Square.

In the morning I was at my desk, doing my routine chores that consisted of making up small items for the movie news columns, and I was summoned to Joe Finston's office. I went upstairs and waited to be admitted.

"Hello, Jim," he said. "Sit down. Two things. First, I'd like you to look this over and see if there's a story in it. It's about me when I was managing a theatre out in Rockaway. It has some amusing stuff in it about how I started in the industry. Don't read it now. I just sort of batted it out because I thought it'd be kind of amusing. The other matter is this Sears dame. We're getting ready to give her the old heave-ho. The key cities are howling bloody murder over her last two pictures and I got nothing but telegrams from all over the country. 'Don't give us any more Sears pictures,' is what they unanimously agree. I don't know what those production guys can be thinking of. I think some of them get softening of the brain from that California sunshine. I can tell you, from my experience as an exhibitor, this dame is costing us. You should see what her last two or three did, the grosses."

"Well, two costume pictures in a row," I said.

"Costume pictures are all right if they make money, but they don't with her in them. What I want you to do, I don't want this dame to have a line, not a line, as long as she's in New York. Cancel all interviews and don't give out any releases on her. I don't care if she climbs the Statue of Liberty, marries the Prince of Wales, she gets no publicity through this office. If you want to plant it that she's on the way out, the gossip writers are all friends of yours."

"Whatever you say, Joe. But I can't ask the gossip writers for any more favors just now. They're laying off the Hunterden story."

"What Hunterden story? Thomas R. Hunterden?"

"Yes, and Sears."

"Our Sears? Charlotte Sears and Hunterden? I don't know about that story. You have to enlighten me."

"Well, now you've got *me* confused. I thought she was all set here because she's Hunterden's girl friend."

"The first I knew about it," said Finston. "Where did you hear it from?"

"I didn't *hear* it. He was there to meet her at the station, the day she came in. And he called her up while I was with her at the hotel. He's married, but I don't know why the gossip writers don't hint at it."

"You saw him at the station?"

"Did I? You should have seen him scatter when he saw those photographers."

"You positively couldn't be mistaken?"

"Not a chance. Thomas R. Hunterden was born in my home town. Gibbsville, P A. Look him up."

"Does she admit it, Sears? I mean about being his girl friend?"

"Oh, sure. She has nothing to lose."

Finston removed his glasses and chewed on the tortoise shell. "Then it's true, eh?"

"What?"

"Well, you hear things and half the time you don't pay any attention, the rumors and gossip you hear." He was trying to lie his way out of his ignorance of the Hunterden-Sears affair, and doing it so badly that I was almost embarrassed for him. He looked at his watch, and I knew he was reckoning the time on the Pacific Coast. "Tell you what you do, Jim, you read that material I gave you and let me know what you think of it. I'll let you know later about the Sears publicity. I still want to think it over a while longer."

"Whatever you say, Joe." I went out, and I stood a moment to light a cigarette near his secretary's desk. Finston's voice came through the intercom.

"Get me Mr. Morrie in Hollywood," he said. "Home, if he isn't at the studio."

I could have been quietly noble about what I had done for Chottie Sears, but she needed some good news and I had it for her. It amused her, too, that I had accidentally but quite truthfully been able to make use of the two men who were giving her the most trouble, to play them against each other without telling a lie. "You know who would have enjoyed this was my grandfather, Pat Somerville," she said. "Did you ever hear of Pat Somerville? An old-time song-and-dance man. And playwright. He wrote dozens of plays and acted in many of them. A good Mick, like yourself, and it was always a feast or a famine for him and my grandmother. Unfortunately it was all famine by the time I came along, and I never got the benefit of any of the feast. But my mother had a lot of wonderful stories about him. One day they'd be putting on the ritz with servants and horses, and the next day men would come and start moving the furniture out of the house." She paused and studied a diamond ring she was wearing. "My mother used to tell me those stories, but she had more spunk than I have. My father—they had an act together—lit out and left her stranded in Pittsburgh without a nickel and she never heard from him again. He took all their money and her diamond ring. In those days show people used to put their money in diamonds when they were working, and of course hock them when there was a long layoff. They boarded me in a house in Brooklyn in those days, so I could go to school. She got back to New York and partnered up with another man and went out again doing the same act. All she said to me was that my father was taken sick with consumption and in a sanitarium. Being a show-business kid, I'd often heard of that. TB was very common among show people, and I guess I cried a little but my father had never been much to me. Or me to him. My mother'd make him come to see me in Brooklyn when they'd lay off during the summer, but he never tried to pretend that I didn't bore him. And the three of us never lived together after I was about eight years old. I was taking violin lessons and it used to drive him crazy when I'd practice, so they always lived in a hotel and I went on boarding in Brooklyn.

"Finally, when I finished eighth grade my mother and her partner got Willard K. Frobisher to write them a new act that I could be in. Songs, dances and witty sayings, and me on my fiddle doing a toe dance. Damn near ruined my legs, that toe-work. Thank God I gave *that* up in time."

"What was the name of the act? Did your mother marry her new partner?"

"The original name of the act was Dowd and Somerville. My real name is Catherine Dowd. Then the new act was Snow and Somerville *introducing* Charlotte Sears. Sears was the name of a face powder my mother used, and Charlotte—just a fancier name than Catherine, and there were thirty-five thousand Kitties, so I became Charlotte Sears. Society people ask me if I have relations in Boston, and out in the sticks they ask me how's Mr. Roebuck. But I was named after a face powder and a famous empress. Who went nuts, didn't she?"

"Yes, I think so."

"Well, I can sympathize with her, the last couple of days. But I feel better now, temporarily," she said. "Anyway, Jim, the story of my life isn't very interesting, but I left out what I really started to tell you. I don't want to be poor. *I* don't want to be stranded in Pittsburgh. I haven't got as much spunk as my mother. Not that I *am* poor. When I began earning my own living at fifteen, I saved something out of every week's pay. I never missed a week. Never. No matter where I was, I'd go to the post office and send back a money order, even if it was only two or three dollars. There was a bank here that show people used to use for that. So I'm not poor. But it isn't only the money. It's something else. All the years I've been in show business, every new job paid me more money than the last one. I've never taken a cut, and I've never taken a job that didn't pay me more than I'd been getting. That's why I'll fight Finston. It isn't only Finston I'm fighting. It's—oh, hell, you know what it is. Do I have to say it?"

"No."

"Do you know the picture I turned down? Do you know the story?"

"No, I haven't seen the script."

"I play the mother of a seventeen-year-old girl. That is, I would if I took the picture. I could very easily have a daughter seventeen, but I'm not going to let fifty million people see me playing a mother to a seventeen-year-old girl that everybody knows is twenty-two. Jean Raleigh. I'm not going to play Jean Raleigh's mother, because then the public will think I must be over forty, and I'm not. I may not have ten years to go before I'm forty, but I'm not there yet. And regardless of how old I am, your friend Ellis doesn't think I'm so old. And Junior Williamson called again today. He won't take no for an answer, that one. You know, it's almost as if he were taking advantage of me."

"How so?"

"This way. He's very anxious to see me and I've told him absolutely no. But he's not going to give up. He told me so. Well, last night Ellis took me to that speakeasy on 49th Street, Jack and Charlie's. I'd never been there before, and who should be there but Mr. Thomas R. Hunterden? He was with two other men."

"Did you speak to him?"

"No. But he kept looking at me and at Ellis, and he didn't like it a bit that I was with Ellis. Ellis and I had a quick dinner and left to go to the theatre and Hunterden was still there with the two men. Well, what I'm getting at is, what if I showed up there again tonight, this time with Junior Williamson? Or tomorrow night? Or every night?"

"Why hasn't Hunterden got in touch with you?"

She did not immediately answer me. "You risked your job for me, so I'll tell you," she said. "But this is between you and me and nobody else."

"All right," I said.

"The reason he hasn't *seen* me is because he can't. He's in the middle of the biggest deal he ever made. One of the men he was with last night was an Englishman, and the other one I guess was a Turk. He wore a fez, so I guess he was a Turk. Hunterden told me yesterday that there were some men in town that he was going to have to be with until they left. In fact, he said he wasn't going to let them out of his sight. I thought he was lying, but I guess those were the men."

"Sounds like it," I said. "Then he still loves you?"

"Love? Hunterden would choke on that word. A man like Hunterden doesn't think about love, although I shouldn't complain. It's a long time since I've said it and meant it. Jim, maybe you'll be famous some day and then you'll understand certain things."

"What would I be famous for?"

"Writing, maybe. You have something, or I wouldn't be attracted to you. Politics, maybe. Or you might be head of a studio."

"Well, what is it that I'll understand that I don't understand now?"

"Two people like Hunterden and me. We're very much alike. I don't know anything about him—that is, the kind of things I told you about myself. I've only known him less than a year. He came out to the Coast and I met him and I fell for him. Not love. And not just sex. I didn't even know who he was, but naturally he had to be *somebody*, to be invited to Morrie Rosenbaum's to dinner. I guessed that much about him. I didn't sit near him at dinner, but after dinner he sat with me and the first thing he asked me took me completely by surprise. He said, 'Miss Sears, if you owned the Rosenbaum Studio, what other company would you like to merge with?' I said I wouldn't merge with any, not if merging meant equal partnership. I said I'd go into competition with one particular studio and drive them out of business, and then buy them out cheap. 'How would you do that?' he said. And I told him I'd steal their biggest stars and best directors. He asked me how I'd do that and I said if he'd give me the Rosenbaum Studio and plenty of money I'd show him how. Well, he wanted to know how I'd go about getting a certain star. I won't tell you her name. Miss Smith. How would I go about getting Miss Smith, who was under contract to a certain other studio? I said in that particular case I wouldn't go after Miss Smith herself, I'd go after a certain cameraman. It isn't so much that he's one of the famous cameramen, but if Miss Smith ever made a picture without him, she'd soon find out that fifty per cent of her success in pictures is due to him. She'd see herself photographed by someone else, and she'd follow the cameraman as soon as she could.

" 'Very interesting,' he said. Then he wanted to know who I'd keep if I suddenly got control of the company, and I said in other words he wanted to know who I'd fire. 'Not quite,' he said. So I told him I'd keep Morrie Rosenbaum, because he was more interested in making pictures than in the stock market.

"Then he made his first personal remark. He said, 'You know, Miss Sears, there's enough for everybody in this business, but if you and I had known each other ten years ago, we could have had most of it.'

"And I said, 'Well, Mr. Huntington, let's take what's left.' I thought his name was Huntington.

" 'No,' he said. 'Let's take our share, and then look into other possibilities, and see what we have ten years from *now*.' That particular moment was when Ruth Rosenbaum decided everybody ought to play poker. It was all right. I won about two thousand dollars, but I didn't see Hunterden alone till four or five days later. A Sunday noon. He came to my house unannounced, without calling up in advance. He came down to the pool, where I was reading the Sunday papers, and he said, 'Am I too late for breakfast, or too early for lunch?' He stayed till Tuesday afternoon, and then he had to go back to New York. Incidentally, Wednesday or Thursday of that week I saw in the trade papers that Guy Smallwood had just signed a new contract with the Rosenbaum Studio. He was the cameraman. You can guess who the star was."

"Oh, sure. She's with us now."

"And getting a picture I wanted to do."

"But I'm surprised that Morrie Rosenbaum didn't know about you and Hunterden."

"We never went out together in Hollywood, and the few times we went to speakeasies in New York, other people were along with us. Hunterden has a deadhead that works for him, and if anybody saw the four of us out together they wouldn't know whether I was with Hunterden or his straight man."

"You started to tell me you and Hunterden are very much alike, then you got sidetracked."

"We are. If I were a man I'd be the same way with Charlotte Sears as he is. I understand where I fit into his life and where I don't. In fact, I don't have to be a man to understand all this. If I were on the crest of the wave, I might be treating Hunterden the way he's treating me. But I'm not on the crest of the wave. I have things worrying me, and when that happens I'm not as sure of myself. No spunk. I'm best at figuring things out when the heat's not on me. Hunterden has this big business proposition bothering him, and he doesn't want to be bothered with a woman too till it's all settled." She smiled. "I wish you were just a moron. Then you could make love to me and I could forget about Hunterden. But if you were a moron I wouldn't want you to make love to me."

"I'm very close to making love to you right this minute."

"I know, and it's exciting. But we better not, Jim."

"If it means so little, why not? Who'd know?"

"I would. The next man that I let make love to me— you don't know what I'm like. I try to run your life, I'm jealous."

"You're not with Hunterden."

"No, because I'm afraid of him. There ought to be another word for love, for people like Hunterden and me. Attraction. Respect. Success. I'm successful, a star. He respects that in me and we're attracted to each other. I know he's a big shot, a star in his own line. So there's a strong attraction that leads to sex. Well, I won't knock sex. I've had affairs that were nothing else and I've stayed up all night waiting for that phone to ring, just like anybody else. But with Hunterden—if I'd refused him on the sexual side, he wouldn't have bothered with me any more, but sleeping with me wasn't all he wanted. I suppose you might say I'm like one of his businesses, but I'm more than that to him and yet it isn't love.

"I don't know about love, anyway, Jim. I've been in love, all the symptoms. Happiness and thrills and desperation. Once I had them change my bookings so I could be on the bill with a magician I was in love with. Oh, he was a bad man, too."

"Did he want to saw you in half?"

"You think you're joking, but he gave me a beating one Saturday night in Baltimore that I never thought I'd make the Monday matinée in Philly. I had to wear black tulle over my arms and shoulders, and I had a mouse under my eye that I had to have leeches for. I was doing a single and up to the last minute I wasn't sure I could go on. But then I saw him grinning at me and I said to myself, 'You so-and-so, you go out there and wow them, and that'll show him.' I did, too, although I was half dead."

"No spunk, eh?" I said.

"Oh, I'll fight. By no spunk I mean I don't have the endurance that my mother had. The long pull, as they say down in Wall Street."

"I think you underestimate yourself all around," I said.

"Not to hear me talk about what a success I am," she said. "Well, a week from now and I'll be getting off the train at Pasadena, with a lot of new clothes and probably a whole trunkful of new headaches. I have two more days in New York."

"How do you figure that?"

"I'm going away for the weekend. To Long Island," she said. She waited for me to say something, but I remained silent. "You won't ask me where?"

"It's none of my business," I said. I could not keep the huffiness out of my tone, and she laughed.

"I like to tease you," she said.

"In more ways than one," I said.

"Oh, now that's not fair. I didn't tease you the other way, and I could have."

"You didn't do so well with Finston," I said, knowing as I said it that it was a cruel and vicious thing to say; but I had no control over, no knowledge of the depth of, the frustration I felt.

She looked at me very calmly. "After that remark you can't stay here any longer," she, the movie queen, said.

I got my hat and coat out of the foyer closet and went down the hall and pushed the button for the elevator. I put on my coat and watched the indicator as the elevator climbed and then began its descent. It was two or three stories above me when I heard her voice. "Jim? Come on back."

I went back and she was holding the door open for me. She closed it behind me and stood leaning against it. We looked at each other and then as naturally as we breathed we embraced, and I kissed her. She reached back her hand and turned the deadlatch. "It's what you want, isn't it?" she said.

"Very much," I said.

"Then I do too," she said.

I had seen, as a hundred million others had seen, the outlines of her body many times, but the extraordinary beauty of it as I saw her in the next few minutes was beyond my past imaginings. There was no bad disposition or sorrow in her love-making; she was pleased and she was happy to be pleasing. I think she was glad to be friends again, to heal the hurt I had inflicted on her and to do so by an ultimate generous act of her own, without waiting for me to express my regret, without pausing to forgive.

I was young, not inexperienced, but young, and my experience counted for little in this new lesson. I was learning for the first time that a woman could be gracious in a calculated act of love, that she could deny the pleasure to many who wanted it, who even wanted to trade love for it, but that she could make a present of pleasure and of the honor of her trust without asking for promises or tokens. Both of us knew that this would not happen again, and that her earlier warning to the next man who might make love to her did not now apply. I had enjoyed what she gave, she had enjoyed the giving. She lit a cigarette for me and asked me if I wanted to sleep, and as she sat on the edge of the bed she seemed reluctant to get dressed again.

"Don't you want to go to sleep?" I said.

"Oh, no. But you can. I'll let you sleep for a half an hour." She took my cigarette and inhaled once, then put it out in the ash tray. "I'll remember this when you're famous," she said.

"I'll have you to the White House," I said.

She shook her head. "No, this is just between us, you and me. You did a lot for me out of niceness, and I couldn't let you think I was a teaser."

"I didn't think that."

"You might have. You did. You thought I was teasing you about the weekend, and I guess I was. Yes, I was. I didn't think I was, but I was. Don't be stubborn, Jim. Ask me where I'm going."

"Where are you?"

"The Williamsons'."

"The father and mother's?"

"No, Junior's house. His wife invited me."

"I didn't know you knew her."

"I don't. At least I've never met her. Have you met her?"

"Hell, no. Or him either. I don't know those people. I only know Ellis through a speakeasy that's open in the morning."

"From something Ellis told me, Junior's wife is quite desperate. And she's pretty clever, too. Junior has his next wife picked out, according to Ellis, and the present one I *think* would like me to break that up. She knows I had an affair with Junior, and I guess she thinks the next Mrs. Williamson won't like it a bit if I show up again. You're not listening. Go to sleep."

"I heard every word you said," I said, and then I dozed off.

It was dark and the traffic sounds of early evening in New York—the beep horns, the protesting second speeds of the buses, and the cab starters' whistles—brought me back to consciousness. Charlotte Sears in negligee and panties, was sitting at her dressing-table. "You rejoining the party?" she said.

"Where's your maid?"

"She'll be here in a little while. I couldn't hide anything from her, so I don't try. I had your suit pressed."

"Have I got a date with you tonight?"

"Well, I have theatre tickets and I have no other date."

"Fine."

"You can do me a great favor, if you will. Have you got a car?"

"No."

"Well, will you hire one and drive me out to the Williamsons' tomorrow afternoon?"

"Sure."

"She offered to send a car for me, but I want to do it my way. If I feel like getting the hell out of there, will you come out and rescue me?"

"Of course."

"Hunterden phoned while you were asleep."

"I thought I heard you talking."

"You didn't hear a thing. You were really out. Anyway, he wants to see me Sunday night, in town, so even if I don't call you before then, will you come out and get me Sunday afternoon?"

"Sure."

"Finston has lost," she said.

"Good work. Did you find that out from Hunterden?"

"I sure did. Morrie called Hunterden from the Coast and said he had good news for him. The Studio was giving me the lead in *Rhapsody on Broadway,* a musical that I'm dying to do. Morrie giggled and said he just thought Hunterden would like to know. Hunterden was taken completely by surprise, but he wasn't annoyed. In fact he was pleased. But the man that really swung the whole thing—little old you."

"Great," I said. "Tomorrow I'll watch Mr. Finston crawl."

"I'm going to do something worse. I'm not going to answer the phone when he rings. I'll let him hang for a week. But doesn't that please you, how it worked out?"

"It certainly does."

"And yesterday I was down at the bottom of the bottomless pit. Do you like champagne?"

"Not much."

"But let's have some tonight, even if we don't drink it all."

"Company money," I said.

"What kind of a car would you like? I mean to own?"

"Don't buy me a car, Chottie. It'd be a waste of money."

"All right, then, not a car, but I'm going to give you something. You wouldn't wear a diamond ring, would you?"

"No."

"How about a trip to Europe?"

"Well, it would be fun to go as a passenger. I've been to Europe, but I worked my way."

"The *Ile de France?* Would you like that?"

"Who wouldn't?"

"You decide when you want to go, and the boat, and I'll pay your fare both ways and all your hotel and travel expenses for a month. Can you get a leave of absence?"

"I don't know, but it won't make the slightest difference. I'll just go."

"Just tell me when, and the trip is yours."

"Thank you."

We had dinner at Jack and Charlie's. It was a small room, low-ceilinged, and no table would seat more than six comfortably, but it was the best speakeasy in New York; the food was excellent, and there were many rumors to explain the high quality of the liquor, the recurring one being that certain highly placed financiers had got Andrew Mellon to allow the Bermuda rum-runners to slip through the Coast Guard patrols. Everything was expensive, and I seldom went there when I was not spending company money.

"Over in the corner, the table that's hidden by the bar," said Charlotte Sears.

"Who?" I said.

"Hunterden and the Turk and the Englishman. Now he sees me." She bowed. "Might as well speak to him if Morrie knows about us. He's coming over."

Thomas Rodney Hunterden, expensively tailored in a black suit and wearing a black silk necktie with a smoked pearl stickpin, shook hands with Chottie. "How do you do, Miss Sears," he said.

"Hello, Mr. Hunterden. I saw you here last night but you didn't recognize me. Will you join us? This is Mr. Malloy, of our publicity department."

"Could I sit with you for a minute?" He included me in the question, but he did not wait for my answer.

"I've seen you before, haven't I, Mr. Malloy?"

"Well, I get around," I said.

"What part of the country do you come from?" he said.

"I come from a place called Gibbsville, Pennsylvania."

"Oh, yes. In the coal regions."

"Oh, you've heard of it?"

"I was born there, but I left when I was very young."

"You two were born in the same town?" said Chottie.

"But I persuaded my parents to take me away when I was two years old," he said. It was not very funny, but it was a remark that put me in my place. "I saw your picture in the paper, Miss Sears. Will you be in town long?"

"Leaving for the Coast Monday."

"Well, I hope we run across each other again. Nice to see you. I have a very good friend in your organization, Mr. Malloy. Remember me to him if you see him."

"Who's that, and I will?"

"Morrie Rosenbaum. Have to get back to my friends." He rejoined the Turk and the Englishman.

"Dying to know who you were," said Chottie.

"And to make sure I didn't get any ideas. He has a very good friend in my organization."

She patted my knee. "Don't let him annoy you. After all, two hours ago."

"What do you think kept me from telling him to go to hell?"

"Me."

"True," I said.

"You can be as independent as you please, but I can't."

"But you are."

"No, I'm not. I cheated with you, Jim, but he's my big moment. He always will be. We didn't find a word to use instead of love, but whatever it is, that describes it. And it's the same with him. He had to know who you were."

"Why not call it love, Chottie? Nobody's going to fine you for misusing the word."

"You get over love. I won't get over this."

"Then you're worse than in love."

"Oh, I know that. That's what I've been trying to tell you."

"I'm a very unimportant guy," I said. "He didn't have to threaten me by telling me what good pals he is with M. R."

"He shouldn't have done that, but he couldn't help it. And don't forget, Jim. His instinctive jealousy was right. Where were you and I two hours ago? The man is no fool."

"I never thought of it that way."

"The same instinct that made him pick me out at Ruth and Morrie's dinner party. He said to me one time, the secret of his success was to find out everything he could about, well, about a business. Get all the facts, and then play his hunches, even when the facts seemed to lead in another direction. Just now he followed a hunch. Maybe I was sitting too close to you, or enjoying myself too much. But he had a hunch, and he was right. Although he'll never know he was right."

"Yes, but maybe he'd be jealous of anybody."

"He wasn't jealous of Ellis. There goes that rhyme again. He saw me with Ellis, but he didn't come to the table. He had no hunch about Ellis, and he did about you. Give him credit." She paused. "Also, I don't like to say this, but watch your step. I'm going to lie to him when he asks me about you, but he may not believe me, although he'll pretend he does. And he might make up some other excuse to have you fired."

"Oh, he wouldn't do that to another Gibbsville boy,"
I said.

Abruptly Hunterden rose and came over to our table
again. "Have you and Mr. Malloy been to the Florence
Club, the Chez Florence? I'm taking my friends there
later if you'd care to join us. About two o'clock? It
doesn't start till late, or is that no news to Mr. Malloy?"

"I've been there quite a few times," I said.

"Miss Sears?"

"All right, fine," she said.

"I see you're just finishing dinner, so I infer you're
going to the theatre. Two o'clock, then? Splendid." He
went back to his table.

"Well, that was pretty smart," I said.

"Why?"

"Don't you get it? We go to the theatre and we get out
after eleven, probably go some place for a drink, meet
him at two, and stay under his watchful eye till four or
five. The whole evening taken care of, in case I get any
ideas. That was damned smart. And at five o'clock tomorrow morning, or whenever, he'll deposit me right
at my door, in his beautiful big Rolls-Royce."

"How do you know he has a Rolls?"

"There's one parked outside, so I guess it's his."

"It is. I recognized the chauffeur."

I had failed to anticipate the degree of Hunterden's
strategy. At the Florence Club he and his companions
were with three show girls from Mr. Ziegfeld's produc-

tion. The Turk did not drink, but the Englishman and I drank a lot, while Hunterden nursed a highball until about half-past four. Hunterden then made his excuses and departed with Chottie, and the Turk, the Englishman, and I were left with the show girls and Hunterden's Rolls. The girl who got me was sore as hell, as she might well have been, to have had such an unprofitable evening, but at least I got four hours' sleep before going to the office.

I telephoned Chottie. "Do you still want me to drive you out to Long Island?"

"Why? You're not running out on me, are you?"

I laughed. "You're a fine one to be talking about running out. Is everything okay?"

"Blissful," she said, and she meant it. "Will you call for me around five-thirty?"

"Yes. What am I supposed to be, I mean am I your brother or cousin? In case I have to act a part at Mrs. Williamson's."

"You be a devoted admirer that likes to do things for me. That's real type-casting."

"It's a part I like to play, Chottie," I said. I liked this woman in a way and to a degree that probably only another man would understand, although it was a woman—she herself—who had come closest to putting it into words when she declared that you get over love, but you don't get over "this."

I drew some expense money and went up to Co-

lumbus Circle and picked out a second-hand Duesenberg S-J, which was on sale for $18,000. It was a phaeton
with a tonneau windshield. "I want to hire it for the
weekend," I said.

"Not a chance," the salesman said.

"Don't be so hasty," I said. "I want to hire it, and
I don't want to pay you a nickel." I introduced myself
and told the man that I was squiring Miss Charlotte
Sears around Long Island society, and if he didn't want
the publicity, I'd just as soon give it to another car. He
said he'd have to talk to the manager.

"Get me a picture I can blow up and put in my
window, and the car is yours," the manager said. "With
Miss Sears at the wheel, of course."

"Of course," I said.

I then got my coonskin coat out of hock and Charlotte
Sears and devoted friend drove out to the Williamsons'
in style. The Williamson butler was not impressed, but
Mrs. Williamson was. "What a beautiful car," she said.
"Did you drive from California?"

"It isn't my car," said Chottie.

"It's yours, Mr. Malloy?"

"For the time being," I said.

"I've never driven one," said Mrs. Williamson, wist-
fully. "Are you in a terrible hurry? Couldn't the three
of us . . . ?"

The butler removed Chottie's luggage and we went
for a ride out the North Country Road. Polly Williamson

took the wheel, and she was a good driver. On the stretch past the Hutton place she hit ninety m.p.h., and after we turned around she took the same stretch at slightly more than a hundred. Her delight was simple and disarming. "I've never done that before in my life. What a wonderful car. Thank you, Mr. Malloy." She herself was simple and disarming, unlike the person I had expected her to be. She was not pretty by the standards of the three girls I had seen the night before; but she had a good figure and legs, and if her hands had not been strong we would have landed in a ditch. The Duesenberg was not a woman's car, and I guessed that Polly Williamson was accustomed to handling big Irish hunters.

She was wearing a checked suit and was hatless, and her blond hair was in disarray from the spin. When we got out of the car at her house she patted the door and smiled. "Can you come in and have a drink?" she said.

"Thanks, but I have to be on my way," I said.

"I hope I didn't make you late. If you're going to be in the neighborhood why don't you come in Sunday afternoon? Don't call or anything, just come if you can."

I almost hated to leave, and Polly Williamson, by her unexpected friendliness, had made me feel I was welcome to stay. She was in her middle twenties, the age of most of the girls I was taking out at that period of my life. She had two small children, and I knew that she was having trouble with her husband. But where I had been led to expect a neurotic, jealous woman, I could see only a young wife who was making an effort to save her marriage by resorting to the kind of intrigue that I was sure was new to her. I do not wish to imply that I saw her as a simple, suburban housewife; the butler wore silver-buttoned livery; the Junior Williamsons' house was only the second largest on the estate, perhaps a quarter-mile distant from the main house whose chimneys and roofs we could see above the trees on a hilltop; and while we were saying goodbye a toothless little man in breeches and buttoned canvas puttees rode past us on a lathery gelding, leading another horse with the stirrup irons tucked up, on his way to the stables. The little man tipped his cap to Polly Williamson. "Just back, Peter?" she said.

"Yes ma'am, just these five or ten minutes," he said, without halting.

"My husband and a friend of his," said Polly Williamson. "They must have stopped in at the big house, but you sure you can't wait to meet them?"

"Afraid not, but thanks very much, and Chottie, see you Sunday if not before?"

Chottie Sears was grinning at me and my not well-hidden admiration of her hostess. "I hope you can make it Sunday," she said.

"I'll try," I said, and put the Duesenberg in gear. I had plans for the weekend; I was not going to waste the Duesenberg; but I drove away reluctantly. I suppose that at that period I was about as fancy-free as it is possible for a man to be, which in my case, however, meant also that I was ready to fall in love with almost any attractive girl. There was an element of pity in my admiration of Polly Williamson, and that element nullified what would otherwise have been the awesome effect of her possessions.

I took the Port Washington ferry and spent Friday and Saturday nights with friends in Connecticut. At noon on Sunday, while we were having breakfast, I was called to the telephone. It was, of course, Chottie Sears. "Duty calls," she said.

"How's it going?" I said.

"Not so good. Can you get here around five? They're having some people in and I have to stay for that, but I want to be ready to go any time. I'll be packed and everything, so we can leave here before eight. You don't have to play any part. Polly Williamson knows who you are. We've gotten to be friends. Her whole plan collapsed last night after dinner. Junior got plastered and he and his lady friend disappeared about eleven and never came back. We'll see how things are at lunch, but as of now this marriage is a fiasco, and for her sake I'm sorry. She wanted to make it go, but he's a silly, spoiled brat. Wait till you see what took him away from Polly."

The other guests had not arrived when I got to the

Williamsons' house, and without prior information I could not have guessed that all was not serene. Junior Williamson, dressed for town in a blue suit, black shoes, and stiff collar, pretended to me that I had cost him money he could not afford. "My wife wants a Duesenberg just like yours," he said.

"She can have mine, because it isn't mine. I rented it," I said.

"Isn't it a new car?"

"No, it's second-hand. They want eighteen thousand for it."

"That's quite a come-down from the original price, isn't it? Don't they sell for over twenty thousand?"

"Around twenty-two, I think," I said.

"That's a lot of money. I'm in favor of renting cars. I always do when I go abroad."

"Yes, but if people like you don't buy those cars, they'll stop making them," I said.

"No, not really. There'll always be guys like Thomas R. Hunterden to buy them. You know, Thomas R. Hunterden, the holding-company guy?"

"He's coming here this afternoon," said Polly Williamson.

"That's what made me think of him," said Williamson. "Somebody told me he kept a Rolls in New York, one in London, and one in Paris. And they're not rented."

"Well, I suppose a fellow like that can make sixty thousand dollars in one day," I said.

"Easily, but think of the upkeep. My father and I together, I think there are about eighteen cars on this place, with the two small trucks. A ton-and-a-half Dodge truck and a Ford. That may seem like a lot, but we have a full-time mechanic, an absolute genius with cars, and we get a good discount on gasoline and oil, quantity buying. It probably doesn't cost us as much to keep a Pierce-Arrow going as it does some fellow that has one Chevrolet. And I'll bet you—no. I was going to exaggerate. I was about to say we could run our whole garage on what a fellow like Hunterden spends for three cars in three cities. I was thinking about three chauffeurs, garage bills, and so forth. I suppose the actual outlay is less for Hunterden, but our cars are always in use. That's where the big difference is. Every car on this place is in actual use. My mother, my father. My wife. Taking one of the children to school. Servants to church. Marketing. Actually, if we had room in the garage, my father was thinking of buying a horse van *as an economy*. He gets awfully tired of paying a fellow in Roslyn every month for vanning. Five dollars a head, just from here to Meadow Brook."

The fascinating thing about Williamson's monologue was his taking for granted that I shared his problem: I was in his house, I had his highball in my hand, and I therefore was a sympathetic listener. I had once experienced the same blind, uncomplimentary acceptance when I was sent to interview a Princeton professor who

had won a prize for some scholarly research in Sanskrit.
Both Williamson and the professor assumed, without
the courtesy of inquiring into my interests and my ignorance, that their language was also mine. Williamson
had paid no attention to my remark that I was renting
a second-hand car, other than to assume that my reason
for renting a second-hand car would be the same as his
for hiring cars in Europe. If his wife had not been present I would have made a burlesque of his father's per-
secution by the Roslyn horse-vanner, but I did not want
to add to her troubles. I also did not want to kid this
humorless man into giving me a punch in the nose. He
glowed with health and strength; in the downward turn
of the corners of his eyes there were warnings of a bad
temper, and he had the meaty hands of a former oars-
man. Four—six—eight years of rowing gives them a
good fist that they keep all their lives.

Williamson was ready to change the subject, and did.
"It's been awfully nice having Chottie here again," he
said. "Chottie, you mustn't ignore us the way you've
been doing."

"Hollywood isn't exactly around the corner, Junior,"
said Chottie Sears.

"I know, but don't you have to come to New York a
lot?" he said.

"Not often enough," said Chottie.

"Why can't they make their pictures just as well in
New York? I read an article not so long ago, about

making movies over in Long Island City. Ever since the talkies they have to film everything inside a studio, it said. So the California sunshine isn't an advantage any more."

"Real estate," said Chottie. "The picture companies have a lot of money tied up in real estate."

"California bores me," said Williamson. "That everlasting sunshine."

"Go there during the rainy season," said Chottie.

"The what? I didn't know it ever rained there. But I suppose it must sometime."

I was beginning to understand Williamson and his attraction for women. In ten minutes he had proved to me that he was one of the stupidest men I had ever met, but the society girl and the movie queen watched every move he made and attended every trivial word. He would take a sip of his drink, and they would watch the elevation of the glass, the lowering of it, and then their gaze would go back on his face. His wife had hardly spoken a word since my arrival, and I noticed for the first time a phenomenon of her attentiveness: when Williamson was speaking, she would look at his mouth, and her lips would move in a barely discernible, unconscious forming of his words. Polly Williamson was a rich girl in her own right, from a family as rich as the Williamsons, and was therefore not dazzled as Chottie Sears might be by the Williamson fortune. In an otherwise masculine face Williamson had a feminine, cupid'sbow mouth, and I now recalled Chottie's remark about his being a mama's boy. He was indeed a mama's boy, with the mouth of a pubert and the appetites of a man; the brainless cruelty of a child, and the strength to arouse in a woman an urgent need to give him pleasure. With the addition of my own observations I agreed with Chottie's epithet. Williamson also had a rather musical voice, not at all unpleasant, and he spoke in the accent of his class. He would pronounce third and bird as though they rhymed with an r-less beard. Polly Williamson's pronunciations were identical with his and her voice was nicely modulated, so that in the present company the Williamsons' accent and voices were harmonious, while Chottie Sears, deep-voiced and with a smoothed-over Brooklyn enunciation, and I, with a harsh voice and an Eastern Pennsylvania twang, were two soloists against a duet. Our voices, our accents, and we ourselves were out of place in this house, in this room. I cannot say whether I became conscious of our vocal sounds first and of Polly Williamson's silent lip-moving second or that the order of observation was reversed. But my more vivid recollection is of Polly Williamson's lips. Chottie Sears, experienced in turning on and simulating facial expressions, gave no indication of her thoughts while Williamson boldly dismissed the telephone calls he had been making since Chottie's arrival in New York. He correctly assumed that she would play his game in spite of his having shown a preference for another woman the night before.

Williamson was a study of an arrogant aristocrat at work. He represented strength and vitality, three or four generations of careful breeding (with some rather distinguished citizens in his blood lines), and great wealth. He had begun to serve on many boards of trustees that governed the policies of philanthropies and cultural activity of the city and the nation, which had been preceded by his earlier participation in polo and fox-hunting committees and his support of Yale athletics. I had no doubt that he sincerely believed that a seat in the House, to be followed by a seat in the Senate, a Cabinet office and an ambassadorship in London or Paris, all would and should be his. As these things raced through my mind I looked over at Polly Williamson and wanted to tell her that her marriage was safe temporarily: Williamson would not ask for a divorce until his maiden political campaign was over. But I also would have had to tell her that in the event of his defeat (which I regarded as certain), the marriage was finished.

At that point we were joined by a tall, handsome woman of about twenty-eight. I looked at Chottie Sears, who gave me a quick pair of nods, and glanced from the newcomer to Williamson. This, she was telling me, would be the next Mrs. Williamson. Her name, as she was introduced, was Mrs. Underwood; her first name, as she was greeted by the Williamsons, was Eunice.

Eunice Underwood was actually not very tall and not very handsome, but she had chic in abundance. She wore a small black hat with a rhinestone pin on the left side, and as she entered the room she slipped off her mink coat and handed it to a maid, revealing a black satin dress, of which the fringed skirt was cut on the bias. The dress had long, close-fitting sleeves that came down over her wrists. She wore sheer black stockings and black suede shoes that had rhinestone buckles that matched the ornament on her hat. From a platinum chain around her neck hung a large diamond. Two words came to mind: the word dramatic, and the word mistress. I suppose the first word made her costume a success, even though I would not tell her so; and I suppose the second word was in my mind before I saw her, although I might have had the same verbal association without advance preparation. She was black, white, and sleek. Her hard, high little breasts pointed forward against the shiny satin. I had seen breasts like them on an expensive whore: all nipple and little flesh.

She went up to our hostess and said "Hello, Polly," but did not kiss her or shake hands.

"Hello, Eunice," said Polly Williamson.

"Hello, there," said Junior Williamson, exuberantly.

She reached out and smoothed down his necktie. "Hello," she said. "Hello, Miss Sears." She then was silent while I was being introduced, but she looked at me and my ready-made suit during the utterance of our names, and I was out of her life before she said "Howja do." She immediately turned away from me and handed

Williamson an ivory cigarette holder into which he fitted a cigarette from his own case. I suspected that she had made him change to her brand, since there was no discussion over that. She put the holder in her mouth and Williamson lit the cigarette.

"Have you got crowds more people coming, Polly?" she said.

"Between thirty and forty."

"Oh, well, that's not so bad. I'll be able to find a place to sit with only that many."

"Wouldn't some nice gentleman give you a seat?" said Chottie Sears. Polly Williamson suppressed a smile.

"They're not as polite here as I'm sure they must be in Hollywood," said Eunice Underwood. "That reminds me, not that I've seen many films, but I don't think I've ever seen anyone sitting down in one. They're all so busy shooting at each other or throwing pie in each other's faces."

"A lot of them do sit down, though," said Chottie Sears. "There's a trick to it. We call them prat-falls."

"Do you know where your prat is, Eunice?" said Williamson, laughing.

"I can imagine. Where did *you* learn where it is? From Miss Sears?"

Williamson laughed again.

"Steady, girl," said Chottie Sears.

"You two," said Williamson, laughing. "I swear."

A group of six men and women now entered. Three

of the men and one of the women were slightly tight, and Eunice Underwood slowly moved away to a chair in a far corner of the room. "Hey, Eunice," said one of the men.

"Stay where you are, Billy. Don't come over and bother me. You spray people when you're plastered."

"We could do with a little spraying around here," said the woman who was tight, and whom I took to be Billy's wife. A maid brought in a trayful of drinks which apparently had been ordered by the new guests on arrival. The butler stood in the doorway and watched the drinks being served, and then disappeared. Almost immediately another group of six arrived and among them was Charley Ellis.

"Have you been here all weekend?" he said.

"No, I just got here a little while ago," I said.

"I hear there was a bit of a *crise* last night. I thought you might be able to tell me about it."

"Can't tell you a thing," I said. "I was on the other side of Long Island Sound."

"I'll be back after I've said hello," he said. He left me and kissed Polly Williamson and shook hands with Chottie Sears.

Eunice Underwood called to him: "Charles, come here and sit with me a minute."

"I'll sit with you," said one of the other men.

"I didn't ask you, I asked Mr. Charles Ellis."

"I'm giving you your last chance," said the man.

"Is that a threat or a promise?" said Eunice Underwood. "Polly, if I were you I'd tell McDonald to dilute the drinks."

"Oh, I don't think so, Eunice," said Polly Williamson.

"Well, in that case I'm going to have to get tight in self-defense. Junior, get me a martini in a champagne glass, please."

"How'd it be if I got you champagne in a martini glass?" said Williamson, laughing.

"Oh, don't be the life of the party," said Eunice.

Charley Ellis rejoined me. "Where is *Mister* Underwood?" I asked. "Or isn't there any?"

"Eunice's husband? He's feeding the fishes. He got drowned in Bermuda a couple of years ago."

"Oh, that's why she's all in black?"

"No, I don't think that has anything to do with it. She didn't waste many tears on him. Not that he would have on her."

"Has she got a lot of dough?"

"Well, she has enough. But let's just say that if she hooks Junior she'll change her scale of living, not downward."

"Where is she from? She wasn't one of this crowd originally, was she?"

"No, she's from Brooklyn. Her father was a minister."

"Oh, she wants to be a nun," I said.

"I hadn't heard *that*," said Charley. "But I'm told she's tried everything else, and believe me, if she doesn't get

Junior she's going to have to change her scene of opera·
tions."

"Not very popular?"

"Well, not with the women. Decidedly not with the
women. Most of these people have known each other
all their lives. Some of them were engaged to be married and married somebody else, but it's a closed corporation, and Eunice, the complete outsider, married
Buddy Underwood and played it straight for a while.
But she was in too much of a hurry. You can't hurry
these people. They've been together too long."

"What was she in a hurry to do?"

"Oh, I suppose get rid of Buddy and make a better
marriage. If she'd stuck by Buddy, who wasn't much
good, she'd have gotten ahead faster. But instead she
went after the men. She's a good rider, and she used
that, and she's quite a good tennis player."

"She doesn't look the athletic type."

"She is, though. Don't let that slinky get-up fool you.
She rides sidesaddle, and in a top hat and skirt she's
even more impressive than she is today. Plenty of guts,
too. And knows she's hated. Junior is sort of her last
chance, and she knows that. If she doesn't land him, she
knows she'll have to clear out. She gets invited every-
where because nobody wants to snub the next Mrs.
Junior Williamson, but this is the ninth inning, two out,
nobody on base, and she's at bat. A scratch single isn't
going to do it for her. She has to knock one out of the
ball park."

"Why is she after you?"

"After me? She isn't after me. Polly's my cousin, and Eunice would like to line up a few of Polly's relations on her side. She isn't after anybody but Junior, and everybody in this room knows it. That's why I asked you about last night. If she had an open spat with Polly, that would cook her goose for fair, because Junior doesn't want to be hurried. Don't forget, old Mr. Williamson and Mrs. Williamson are still very much alive. Junior takes Eunice to their house every chance he gets, but the old boy and Mrs. Williamson like Polly and they're crazy about those grandchildren."

"Why would Thomas R. Hunterden be invited here this afternoon?"

"I didn't know he was. That'll be a new face, and you don't see many of them in this house. He'd never be asked to the big house, so I guess Junior invited him."

"Why not Polly?"

"Well, anything's possible. Let's see if Alice comes with him. If she does, then it just means that Alice and one of her hospitals has been working on Junior and one of his hospitals. I don't know. You see anybody you'd like to make a play for?"

"Yes. Your cousin."

He shook his head. "No. Anything's possible, but I wouldn't like to see you make a play for Polly now. If a son of a bitch like Hunterden wants to, that's different. But not a friend of mine. If on the other hand she ever gets a divorce from Junior, I'll be as helpful as I can."

"Thanks," I said. "I could go for her."

"I think she's about the best we have to offer, and I'd like to see her shake loose from Junior, but she isn't ready to give up. See anybody else?"

"The blonde in the blue tweed suit."

"Mary Day? Can be had. The coast is absolutely clear, there. Billy's forever on the make for Eunice and it makes Mary sore as a wet hen. Hey, Mary."

The girl called Mary Day sauntered over.

"Here's a friend of mine that thinks you're pretty darn attractive."

"Why shouldn't he? I think he is, too. And a stranger in our midst. Where are you from?"

"He's a Pennsylvania boy," said Charley Ellis.

"Oh, God. Another Biddle?"

"No, I'm one of the anthracite Malloys."

"Oh, Scranton. I was in a wedding there once and I never saw people drink so much—except here, of course. But somehow it shocked me to see out-of-town people do it. Maybe you were at the wedding. It was—"

"I'm not from Scranton. I'm from Gibbsville."

"Oh, Gibbsville. Well, I know a girl that lives *there*. Caroline Walker, married to somebody called English. I spent one god-awful year at Bryn Mawr and she was one of the few bright spots. How is she?"

"Well, I saw her the last time I was home. She was looking well."

"She invited me to her wedding and I invited her to

mine. End of correspondence, but I liked her. She was very nice to me. You give her my love when you see her. Mary Patterson. Can you remember that?"

"Mary Patterson. Sure. I'll remember."

"Are you visiting Charley? I didn't see you at lunch, did I?"

"I'm squiring Charlotte Sears."

"Oh, I want to hear all about her. Is it true that she's going to break up this thing between Junior and Eunice? I *may* have had one too many cocktails, don't you think? I shouldn't drink on Sunday. He who drinks on the Sabbath will live to fight some more. What did you say your name was?"

"James Malloy."

"It won't stick. I've forgotten it already," she said. She was sitting on a sofa between Charley Ellis and me, holding her cocktail glass in both hands. "What did you say it was again? Spell it."

"M, a, l, l, o, y."

"Mallory."

"No, there's no r in it."

"Like oysters."

"Yes. I'm out of season."

"I don't think you are. I think you're very much *in* season, and if you want to know the truth, so am I. You wouldn't like to take me out of here, would you, Mr. Mallory?"

"Where would you like to go?"

"I don't know. I'm open to suggestion."

"I'd love to take you anywhere, if we can be back here by eight o'clock."

"Oh, I don't think we would be. I really don't think we would. In other words, you're spoken for?"

"Not exactly spoken for, but I'm here to drive Miss Sears back to New York."

"Too bad. Or maybe not. Now this old gossip won't have any sleuth. Except that he did hear me proposition you."

"Am I the old gossip?" said Charley Ellis.

"What is sleuth?"

"I thought you were a friend of Caroline's. Sleuth is gossip. An old Bryn Mawr word for gossip. Talk-gossip. But Charley Ellis is a talker-gossip. If you want to know anything about anybody here, ask Charley. Isn't that right, Charley?"

"Just about," said Charley Ellis, not at all offended.

"*But*—if you want to know everything about *Charley*, you have to ask *me*. That's right, too, isn't it, Charley?"

"Just about."

"Ask him something about me," said Mary Day.

"Anything at all?" I said.

"Anything."

"All right," I said. "Has she had her appendix out?"

She laughed. "Go ahead answer him. I want to see what you say. You're in a spot. You don't know whether to be chivalrous or truthful. Go on, Charley, answer his question."

"You answered it for me," said Charley. "I didn't have to say a word—and I still haven't. So stop calling me a gossip, Mary. You get a few too many drinks in you and talk too much, and then you accuse other people of gossiping."

Mary Day turned to me. "Ask me whether *he's* had *his* appendix out? The answer is yes. And have you had yours out, Mr. Mallory?"

"You're not going to find out as easily as that."

"Well said, Jim," said Charley.

"Has Charlotte Sears had hers out?" said Mary Day. "*Why, look at him! He's blushing!* I took him completely by surprise."

"I wouldn't know," I said.

"Oh, come on, it's too late. You got as red as a beet. Why, Mr. Mallory. And you're the one that started this whole thing about appendixes. That's rich."

"You jump to conclusions, Mrs. Day," I said.

She was staring at Chottie Sears, who was sitting between two men, laughing with them and enjoying their admiration. "Some women just have it, that's all," said Mary Day. "I wonder if she ever got tight over some damn man." She got to her feet and slowly, rather shyly, joined Chottie and her admirers.

"She's a swell girl till she drinks, and then—bang! No inhibitions. Says anything that comes into her head, no matter who gets hurt in the process." He was trying, I knew, to avoid the topic of Chottie Sears and me, but he believed Mary Day had made a discovery and he was resentful of it. He had his masculine pride, and I was his successful, deceitful rival.

"Well, as she herself said, she oughtn't to drink on Sunday," I said.

"Or between Sundays. She does most of her damage on Sunday, because there are more people around. But Sunday isn't the only time she drinks too much. She's another of those girls around here that set their caps for Junior, and who got him? Her best friend, Polly. I know what fixed that, too. Mary gave up everybody else for Junior, wouldn't even let people cut in at dances. No dates with anyone else, and behaving like an engaged girl, although Junior was going his merry way. And as against that possessiveness, there in the background, so to speak, was Polly Smithfield, the logical one, waiting to be asked. And she got asked and Mary didn't. That was some wedding. Mary the maid of honor instead of the bride, eyes red going up the aisle. Tight as a tick at the reception, and eloped with Billy Day the next week. She was back here and settled down before Polly and Junior got back from their wedding trip."

"Day isn't so much, is he?"

"He never used to be, but Junior has helped him along and he's doing very well. He has a seat on the Stock Exchange that I understand Junior put up the money for, and downtown Billy's known as Junior's man. Considering what he would have been without Junior's help, that's nice going.

"You know, when you have forty or fifty million behind you, that money does double service. Triple. Quadruple. For instance, McDonald isn't just a butler. He's Junior Williamson's butler, with forty million behind him. Junior Williamson's tailor isn't just a tailor. He has a forty-million-dollar customer. And downtown, Billy Day is Junior's man and that much closer to the money, even if he never gets his hands on it. I could probably get Junior's business. Polly's my cousin. But I think Polly wants Billy to have it, and in any case I wouldn't want to be known as Junior's man. Or anybody else's. When my father dies . . ." He cut himself off.

"What?"

He shook his head. "Don't know you well enough, Jim," he said, with finality. "If I talk about it, I won't do it."

"You wouldn't tell me if I guessed, would you?"

"No, but I'd be interested to hear your guess."

"You want to write," I said.

"Well, it's an interesting guess," said Charley Ellis. "You're probably not kidding your father one bit."

"Probably not. But time is on his side. The longer he lives, the better the chances that I'll give up any crazy ideas I have."

"Why don't you just up and go?"

"The time to do that was when I graduated from college, and never to have gone downtown at all. That was *my* mistake and where the old man was clever. Hell, look at the guys in this room. At least half of them wish they were doing something else. I could tell you about most of them. Eddie Patterson wishes he could be a guide in Canada. Mike Bell should have been a vet. He studied it at Cornell, but now he's a big trader in oil stocks."

"I always wanted to be something else, too," I said.

"You did? What?"

"A millionaire."

Charley smiled. "Do you mean a million a year, or a million all told?"

"I wasn't greedy. At least, not till you said a million a year."

"There are both kinds of millionaire in this room. See if you can tell them apart."

"I guess I couldn't."

"No, I don't think you could, just by looking. Mike Bell probably has a million-dollar income, and Billy Day probably has around a million capital."

"But why does a guy like Bell give up what he wants to do when he has all that money?"

"It's the system, my boy. Or what I call the system, and you know the old saying. 'Don't buck the system or you're liable to gum the works.' Mike went to St. Mark's and then his father allowed him to go to Cornell and study animal husbandry. Then when he graduated, Mr. Bell told Mike he needed him downtown, just about the way my old man did me. You start going downtown, you get a lowly job as a runner or something, and you want to earn a promotion to prove that you could do it if you wanted to. So you earn that promotion and they give you some responsibility, which you have to fulfill. Pride. Meanwhile you're having a very pleasant time. You have lunch with your friends, go to parties, come out here weekends, get married, start having children. You're in the system. You're part of it. And what you wanted to be, or do, that becomes your hobby. In Mike's case, he's an amateur vet. You see, Jim, the best of these guys would have been good at something else. The others, let's not worry about them. They're the Billy Days."

"And what about the Junior Williamsons?"

"How many are there? Not more than half a dozen. Let's not worry about them, either. They're the royalty, and the others are the nobility, the peerage."

"Where are the commoners?"

"Well, there aren't any, not in this group. Not really *in* this group. Eunice is one, and the only way she'll be anything else is by becoming Junior's wife."

"What if I married Polly Williamson?" I said.

"Well, you wouldn't marry her unless you were in love with her and she was in love with you, and we'd know that. You'd get credit for marrying her in spite of her dough and not because of it. But you could never look at another woman, not even flirt a little. You couldn't start spending her money on yourself. You'd have to get something to do that her money wouldn't help you with. *And* if Polly had an affair with another guy, you'd take the rap. It would all come back to your marrying her for her money. And I wouldn't be surprised if that's why Polly wants to save her marriage. She's a very intelligent girl, and she knows there aren't many Junior Williamsons around."

"This is all based on the assumption that I'd give a damn what people said about me."

"Of course it is."

"Well, I don't."

"Well you damn soon would, my friend," he said. "Where are you and Polly going to live? Here? Then you'd be surrounded by Polly's friends. Gibbsville, Pennsylvania? I'll bet your friends would be tougher on you than Long Island. You may think you wouldn't give a damn about Polly's friends or your friends, but people is what people have to live with. And if you're surrounded by hostile people, your friends or Polly's or strangers, your marriage wouldn't last. Oh, just coming in. A perfect example of the commoner."

"I resent that," I said.

"No you don't," said Charley Ellis.

The newcomer was Thomas Rodney Hunterden, dressed for the Scottish moors in August in a tweed jacket and matching plus-threes, tab garters, and fringed-tongue brogues. "Lord Plushbottom," I said. There were others in the room similarly dressed, but the stiffness had not gone out of Hunterden's suit and shoes, nor out of him.

"New York Yacht Club tie," said Charley.

Hunterden made straight for Polly Williamson.

"No Alice," said Charley.

Most of the men showed that they had met Hunterden or recognized his name, but the only woman who greeted him with any informality was Chottie Sears. To my astonishment Junior Williamson took Hunterden's arm and steered him among the men and women, taking care of the introductions. "Mr. Ellis, and Mr. Malloy," said Williamson.

"Mr. Ellis," said Hunterden. "Mr. Malloy, I've had the pleasure. Did you get home safely the other night, Malloy?"

"Yes, did you?"

His quick anger was beautifully controlled. "Quite safely."

"Hunterden, what will you drink?" said Williamson.

"Sherry, please."

Williamson nodded to McDonald. "Damned sensible, I must say. I ought to stick to sherry. I hate the damn stuff," said Williamson.

"Do you? I don't. I like a glass of sherry at this time of day," said Hunterden.

"I don't even like it in soup. I come of a long line of whiskey drinkers, myself," said Williamson. He again took Hunterden's arm, and said: "Well, have you thought that over?" He piloted Hunterden away from everyone else and the two men sat off by themselves, engaged in private conversation. If I was curious, I was no more so than the other men in the room, who were curious and baffled.

"Be interesting to watch the stock ticker tomorrow morning," said Charley Ellis. "I predict a steady rise in Omega Development. That's one of Hunterden's companies. It'll go up a couple of points between opening bell and twelve-thirty. It'll remain steady while these boys are exchanging information at lunch, and then it'll begin to drop off a little because nobody's going to be able to find out a damn thing and the timid ones will take a quick profit. Would you like to make a few dollars, Jim? I'll put in an order for you first thing in the morning, and sell out at twelve noon."

"Do you know how much money I have in the bank?"

"None, the way you say it."

"None."

"Well, I'd lend you some but not to play the market on a tip I gave you."

"Thanks very much, Charley," I said. "I've never been in the stock market, so I didn't lose anything when the crash came."

"Well, that put you on even terms with a lot of guys that had been in it," he said. "At least we found out that Hunterden isn't here on Polly's invitation, and frankly I'm relieved."

"So am I," I said. "They're still gabbing away, Williamson and Hunterden."

"I'm going to see what I can find out from Polly," he said. "Very little, I'm sure, but I'll have a try at it."

The party had grown in size, but there was no individual or group that I felt would welcome my presence, so I waited alone while Charley Ellis spoke to his cousin. She laughed at something he said and shook her head, shrugged her shoulders. Then she stopped smiling and looked over at me and was confused to see me looking at her. Charley Ellis rejoined me.

"Couldn't get a thing out of her," he said.

"I know. So you changed the subject and told her I liked her."

"Yes," he said.

"But she didn't want to sit with us."

"That's exactly right. Can you read lips?"

"No. I almost wish you hadn't said anything about me."

"Would you like to hear what she said? It was nice," he said.

"Sure, of course I would."

"She said she met you at exactly the wrong time. From that I infer that any other time would have been the right time."

"Excuse me," I said. On an impulse I got up and went to Polly Williamson, who was talking with a man and woman. "May I see you a minute, please?"

We stood alone. "Charley told me what you said."

She nodded quickly.

"I have to tell you this. It may be the wrong time, Mrs. Williamson, and it may not last, and I know I'll never see you again. But I love you, and whenever I think of you I'll love you."

She turned away. "I know, I know. Thank you for saying it. It was dear of you."

I left her then and went back to Charley. "You see," he said. "I couldn't have done that."

"You don't know what I did."

"Yes, I do, Jim. You told her you love her."

"Yes, God damn it, I did."

"Did she thank you? If she didn't, I do, for her."

"Yes, she thanked me. Mrs. Williamson." I laughed. "I don't know her well enough to call her Polly, but I had to tell her I love her. How did you know what I was saying?"

"What else would take possession of a man so completely? What else would you have to say to her that was so urgent? And—what else could make her look the way she did when she was first married to Junior? Oh, that was a damn nice thing to do, to make her feel love again. The existence of it, the urgency of it, and the niceness. How long since any two people in this room had a moment like that? Or ever will? You know who I wish I could say that to, don't you? You must know."

"No, I don't," I said.

"To *her!* To Polly! I've never loved anybody but my first cousin, and I never will. But it isn't because we're first cousins that I haven't told her so."

"Why haven't you?"

"Well, yes, it is because we're first cousins. Closer than friends. Different from brother and sister. But she'd be shocked and frightened if she ever knew what it really is. It happens, and it works out, but when I was eighteen and she was fourteen I was ashamed because she was so young. And then when we got older she fell in love with Junior. So I've never told her. But now you see why I understand how you feel. You can't have her either." He smiled. "It seems to me we have a lot in common. I haven't slept with Chottie Sears, and you haven't slept with Mary Day, and I'd like to sleep with Chottie and you'd like to sleep with Mary. And neither of us will ever get anywhere with Polly. I've got drunk with friends of mine on less excuse than that. Shall we just quietly start putting it away, beginning with two double Scotches?"

"I'll have a double Scotch with you, but I have an eighteen-thousand-dollar car and a two-million-dollar movie queen to deliver safely. If you're going to be in New York tonight, I'll meet you anywhere you say."

"I think this would be a good night to get drunk. Don't you? How about if I go in with you and Chottie?"

"That would be fine. We drop her at the hotel, put

the car in the garage, and start out at Dan's." I stood up. "I'll go over and speak to our friend."

Chottie made room for me beside her on the sofa. "Are you about ready to go?" she said.

"Entirely up to you," I said. "You don't mind if Charley Ellis rides in with us, do you?"

"Not a bit. Love to have him. How soon will you be ready to go?"

"I'm ready whenever you are. I've had all I want of this party, and if I stay much longer I'll only get too plastered to drive."

"You're not plastered now, are you? That's a big drink you have, Jim. And I noticed you jumping up and down and whispering things to Polly. Tell me if you're tight, because I'm scared to death to drive with anybody's had too much."

"No, I'm not tight. But in another hour I might be."

"You don't seem tight, but . . ."

"But what?"

"Well—just suddenly springing to your feet and taking Polly off to one side. You were like a wild man. What made you do that? Whatever you said, it had a big effect on her. First I thought she was going to cry, and then instead of that she turned all smiles. And you hardly know her."

"I told her her slip was showing."

"But it isn't. No, you didn't tell her any such thing. You sure you're not tight?"

"I'm not tight, and I won't take any more till I deliver you at the hotel." I placed my glass on the table in front of us, and she crooked her finger at Hunterden. He said something to Williamson and then came over to Chottie.

"Did you signal me?" said Hunterden.

She made sure that no one was listening, and said: "Can I drive in with you?"

It was obviously an interference with his schedule. "I understood this fellow was to take you in."

"She thinks this fellow is stewed," I said. "Where do you get that this-fellow stuff, Hunterden?"

"Jim," said Chottie. "Please?"

"Hunterden, you're a phony. You don't even tell the truth about where you were born. Where *were* you born, anyway? Not Gibbsville, P A. I know that much. And don't this-fellow me. Nobody ever heard of you in Gibbsville and your name isn't even in the Court House records."

"There's no doubt about it. He is stewed," said Hunterden. "You drive in with me and I'll take care of this nobody tomorrow. One phone call, Malloy."

"Save your crooked nickel. I won't show up at the God damn office." I now knew I was tight; I had not known it before.

"Was your father a doctor?" said Hunterden.

"Yes, my father was a doctor."

"I thought so. I didn't like *him,* either."

"But I'll bet you never told him. If you had, you wouldn't be here."

He turned to Chottie. "This fellow is trying to create a scene, and I don't want a scene here, now."

"Well let's not have one. Take me out of here and stop arguing," she said. "Jim, I don't think I'll ever forgive you for this. You're just impossible. I don't know what ever came over you all of a sudden."

"I'm not used to good booze," I said.

"Come on," said Hunterden. He put his hand under her elbow and they went to speak to Polly Williamson. She turned and said something to McDonald, and I guess he got her luggage from upstairs. Charley Ellis came and sat with me.

"What was that all about?" he said.

"I told him off, and it was damn unsatisfactory. I didn't tell him half the things I wanted to."

"Are you plastered?"

"I didn't think so, but I guess I am."

"Can you drive?"

"Oh, I think I can drive. I'm not that kind of tight. I just want to tell people off, and I'd like to give that Hunterden a crack in the jaw."

"He's twice your age and you have fifteen pounds on him. Don't do that. Don't spoil Polly's miserable party."

"I won't."

"There's something brewing between Junior and

Hunterden, and you could spoil it and Junior would blame Polly."

"Oh, I realize that."

"We'll give them a chance to leave, and then you and I can go. I'll drive."

"All right."

He studied my face. "What came over you?"

"What ever possessed me? I'm like Mrs. Day. I shouldn't drink on Sunday, I guess."

Thirty years later I remember most of that spring as well as I do some things that happened a month ago. In this morning's paper they treated Charlotte Sears rather well. She did not make Page One, but they gave her two-column top heads in the *Trib* and the *Times,* called her an "early Academy Award winner" who had come out of retirement in 1958 to win a nomination for best supporting actress as the mother superior in the Joseph S. Finston production, *Benediction at Dawn.* She was described as the last member of a theatrical family that had been prominent in vaudeville during the Nineteenth Century, who had become an outstanding success in the so-called drawing-room comedies of the Twenties and Thirties. Her career, it said, was abruptly terminated in 1930, when an automobile in which she was riding was struck by a train at a grade crossing in Roslyn, Long Island, and she received facial injuries that disfigured her and forced her into

a long retirement. In the same accident, Thomas R
Hunterden, in whose car Miss Sears was riding, was
fatally injured. Hunterden, a stock promoter (it said),
was facing indictment on six counts of fraudulent con-
version and other charges. His tangled financial affairs
resulted in court action over a period of three years, and
his manipulations were instrumental in bringing about
the creation of the Securities Exchange Act of 1934.
Hunterden, a native of Gibbsville, Pa., was a somewhat
mysterious, publicity-shy figure who had made a fortune
through speculations during the First World War. Later
he sought to gain control of motion picture companies
and at the time of his death he had failed in a last-
minute attempt to enlist the financial support of a
syndicate headed by Ethridge B. Williamson, Jr. During
the investigation of Hunterden's financial affairs Miss
Sears was questioned by the district attorney in an
effort to locate securities worth more than $2,000,000
which could not be accounted for, but no charges were
made against her . . .

I remembered that. I went to the hospital every afternoon and read the morning and afternoon papers to
her. I would sit by the window so that I could see the
print; she would not allow the electric light to be turned
on. There were dressings on her nose and chin, and her
arm was in a cast.

She had other visitors besides me. Polly Williamson
came in at least twice a week. Morrie Rosenbaum made

a special trip from the Coast to tell her not to worry. She could have had more visitors, but we three were the only ones she wanted to see. When Morrie Rosenbaum heard that she was going to be questioned about the missing bonds, he telephoned me from Hollywood. "Mally," he said (at $125 a week I did not rate a correct pronunciation), "Miss Sears don't have none of them hot bonds. I stake my life on it. So I got her a lawyer. Not my lawyer. I got her Percy Goodfellow. You know who *he* is? Lawyer to the biggest firms in Wall Street. Bishops he has for clients. The very picture of integrity and a God damn shrewd man. I told him I want him there every minute they're asking her questions."

"Yes sir," I said.

"Oh, why am I telling you? Because you go to hospital and tell her she don't see no district attorney without Goodfellow being there every single minute. You understand? She can't talk to me over the phone, you understand, so you give her my instructions. You tell that little lady we don't want her worrying about a thing. Mally?"

"Yes sir?"

"Tell her love from Ruthie and Morrie. Ruthie is Mrs. Rosenbaum, my wife." He then hung up.

I was never there when Polly Williamson came to see her, but I always knew when she had been there, and not only by the flowers that she continued to bring on every visit. She would stay only ten minutes—a total of twenty minutes a week—but Chottie would always have something to say about her. "It took me a couple of weeks before I got over something," said Chottie.

"What was that?"

"Wishing she wouldn't come. I didn't want her coming here because she felt guilty, because if I hadn't gone to her place this never would of happened. I didn't want you coming for that reason, either. But with you— well, maybe you had another reason."

"I did blame myself," I said. "It was the first thing I thought of when I read about it. If I hadn't got drunk—"

"I know. But you had a man-and-woman reason for coming. I'm in your memory-book. And you're in mine, too, Jim."

"I hope so."

"But Polly doesn't blame herself. I don't think she ever did. She comes here because the night before it happened, when Junior went off with that Underwood dame, Polly knew I was mad as hell at Junior being so insulting. So crude. He was crude. But now when Polly comes to see me, she only stays ten minutes, but she always makes me feel that if she were here instead of me, she'd want me to visit her. Do you see what I mean? She'd *want* me to come. And I've never had another girl that was that kind of a friend. Even if I look like Lon Chaney when I get out of here, it won't all be a total loss."

Another time she said: "Polly was here earlier this

afternoon. She came today instead of tomorrow because Etty, the boy, has to go and have his tonsils out tomorrow, poor kid. A wonderful mother, that Polly. But am I glad I don't have children. If I'd of married any of those hambo boy friends of mine—present company excepted—I'd of wanted children. But if I had a son or a daughter waiting for me to get out of here, I just couldn't face them. The first time they'd see me with my face all banged up. I read something one time about Helen of Troy, if she had a nose that was different by a fraction of an inch, it would have changed the history of the world. Well, mine's going to be different, but it sure as hell isn't going to change the history of the world."

My reading to her was usually confined to the theatrical and movie news and reviews, book reviews, the gossip columns, the principal news stories, and occasionally the sail-and-arrive items on the society pages. "Ah, Eunice Underwood sailed yesterday in the *Ile de France*, to be gone a year," I said.

"No matter how I look when I get out of here, I'll have a better figure than she ever had," she said. "I had a lovely figure."

"And still have."

"I wonder what I'll do about that? Oh, I guess I'll find somebody."

She was depressed.

"They're all the same from the top row in the balcony,"

1, Cleopatra, nay?

she said. "They're all the same with a bag over their heads. I saw a comedy bit in a two-reeler one time. The comic, I forget who it was, he sees this girl in a one-piece bathing suit, great figure, and he follows her up the beach and tries to pick her up. Then when she turns around she has a face like Bull Montana. The comic did a Bobby Vernon grando and ran. I don't think it's as funny now as I did when I saw it. Now don't give me false encouragement."

"How do you know I was going to give you any?"

"Because I can see you, even if you can't see me. And you were going to say something encouraging. Don't. They're gonna do what they can, the doctors. I'll have a different nose, and they've got this wire in my jaw. I'll be able to put make-up over the scar in my cheek. I was thinking of changing my name and starting out playing character bits, but everybody'd know it was me. That'd be too good a story for you boys in publicity."

"It would get around, even if we laid off."

"Yes, and the last thing I want is stuff about brave little Charlotte Sears. If I have to be brave I don't want to be brave in public."

"You have spunk, just like your mother."

"That's one satisfaction. I'm beginning to get over my inferiority complex about her. But I'm only—well, I'm under forty, and I hope and pray I find a good man. God protect me from gigolos. God keep me from paying a man to sleep with me."

She in her wisdom had thought it all out, the danger she faced that had been my secret worry for her. We both knew actresses who kept gigolos, and we knew that the gigolos laughed at them and that some of the actresses even made cruel jokes at themselves.

"You have plenty of money," I said. "Look around and get something to do."

"Don't think I haven't thought about that. I could be an agent. I know this business cold, and I have the contacts. A lot of things I *could* do, like being a script girl. Wardrobe. But I was a star, and I don't need the money. I've been trying to think what I could do out of show business entirely. I wish I'd gone to high school, then I could go to college and study to be a doctor. I guess I'll get over that as soon as I get out of here, but it was one idea I had. Open a shop, but I'd soon get tired of that. Interior decorator. Doesn't interest me."

"Charity work," I suggested.

"No. I'm too accustomed to making my own living. I have to do something I'll be paid for, even if it isn't much at first. By the way, Jim. You're still going to take that trip to Europe."

"No."

"Yes. I didn't mention it before because I needed you here. But in another three or four weeks I'll be going back to the Coast."

"I don't want to go to Europe. As soon as you leave I'm quitting Rosenbaums'. I start a new job the first of

August. Second-string dramatic critic. It's a job I want.
Pretty good pay, and time to start writing a novel."

"Morrie's paying my bills here, you know, so it isn't
a question of money."

"Be honest, Chottie."

"Well, I'll tell you. Morrie is paying all my bills and
I'm letting him do that. He really wants to, and I want
him to. It makes him feel good, he and Ruthie. But of
course I'm through at the Studio. I'm going to sell my
house and have that money for capital. The money I've
invested will keep me the rest of my life, not in luxury,
but comfortably. I'll get a little house out in the Brentwood section for me and my maid, and I'll live quietly
out there. Morrie told me I'd never have to worry about
money, and he's one that keeps his word. Well, if he
gives me as much every year as I have been getting
every week, finances won't worry me. Morrie says he'll
figure out a way to keep me on the payroll. Story department, most likely. He knows I'm a great reader, and if
I give them one story idea a year, like suggesting a
magazine serial they ought to buy, I'll be earning my
pay."

"You certainly will."

"There's one thing I've always been interested in and
it's why I always used to go for walks. Remember me
telling you I used to go for those long walks when I
was on the road? You know, in most towns I played, if
you walk steadily for fifteen-twenty minutes, you're out

of the business section and you start getting in the residential."

"It's only about a hundred-yard dash where I come from."

"Yes, it varies with the size of the town. But when you get out of the built-up section, you come to the thing that interested me the most. Hold on to your seat."

"I'm holding on."

"Flowers. I love flowers. I used to ask the stagehands who had the best gardens in every town I went to. The wise-guys used to ask me if I meant beer gardens. Sometimes I'd take the trolley to look at a garden, if it was too far out to walk. If there was a real famous one, big, I'd even take a taxi. I have over a hundred books on flowers and gardening. You know, Polly Williamson I discovered knows a lot about flowers, but I have to admit, I know more. You know, most flowers have at least two names. Different names in different countries, like larkspur for delphinium, bachelor's button for cornflower. That's in addition to the Latin names. I never got as far as Latin, so I don't know many Latin names, but I guess I've learned about fifty, the more common flowers. Our California flowers—" She halted. "That's enough of that. When I start talking about our California flowers. Do you know who loved flowers?"

"Who?"

"Loved flowers, and had a great knowledge of them. Tom Hunterden. A discovery we both made by accident. One day he was at my house and he got up and walked over slowly toward one of my rose bushes. 'What's the matter?' I said. 'Do you see a snake?' Up where my house is we get rattlers. 'No,' he said. 'This is a hybrid tea rose, and I've been thinking of putting them in at home.' We didn't spend *all* our time talking about picture business, Jim. Even if you didn't like him, he was a fascinating man."

"Why were you afraid of him? You told me once you were."

"I wasn't afraid of him. But he inspired fear in me. It wasn't only the fear of losing him. It was just fear, Jim. A lot of times just thinking about him would make me afraid of something, I didn't know what. He believed in hunches himself, and hunches are nothing but intuition. I had the same thing after I got to know him. Not hunches. But intuitive fear."

"A premonition?"

"Yes, I guess it was, considering what happened. When I came to New York this last time, when he didn't meet me at the station, I was upset but I was relieved. I thought maybe he and I were through and I'd get over this fear I had. I was glad to make love with you, because that showed me that I wasn't hypnotized by Hunterden. But I guess maybe I was hypnotized by him, if you remember later that night. By the way, did you sleep with that show girl?"

"No."

"She was a real gold-digger. She was a Ziegfeld edition of Eunice Underwood. That's one thing nobody could ever say about me. Will you write to me, answer my letters if I write to you?"

By agreement I did not see her off when she left the hospital, and I did not know the condition of her face. She took the less fashionable trains, and had reservations under fictitious names. Ruth Rosenbaum met her in Los Angeles and helped her to find the house in Brentwood that she bought as Catherine Dowd. With make-up to cover the scar, she did not look too awful unless you remembered the original, but in the new house she had no photographs of herself before the accident, and she was gradually trying to get used to the new face and the old name. All this I learned in her occasional, chatty letters, which came less frequently as time went on. Brentwood was not fancy enough for the movie stars who were buying and building in Beverly Hills, although Greta Garbo lived not far from Chottie's house. "She vants to be alone and so do I," wrote Chottie, "but I really am. I went shopping in Santa Monica and nobody recognized me. I have not got up nerve enough to shop in Beverly but I will."

Then one day, about a year after the accident, she wrote that she had bought a greenhouse, which she was calling Dowd & Company, and her letters became few and far between. We exchanged Christmas cards, but I stopped hearing from her until 1934, when my novel was published and she sent me some California reviews. She had bought a copy of the book but had not had a chance to read it but would read it before I got to California, which she knew would be as soon as she had read that I had signed with Paramount.

I drove out to have dinner at her house and I realized on the way that I had never seen her face after the accident. I found her house with some difficulty. The place was surrounded by an eight-foot hedge that gave her complete privacy, and since I knew I was to be the only guest for dinner, I parked my car in the short driveway and rang the front doorbell.

She opened it herself, swung it wide and stood smiling.

"Would you have recognized me?" she said.

"Not immediately, not unless you spoke." I kissed her and she hugged me.

"You don't have to be careful what you say. I'm all right. It's so good to see you again. You're older, and more attractive that way. You've been married and divorced, and you've written a fine book, and what kind of a deal did you make at Paramount?"

"One of those seven-year option things. I signed the first contract they offered me because I wanted to get out of New York. How is Dowd & Company?"

"Doing very well. It was tough in the beginning, but I survived the first year, and the second year I just about broke even on the business, and now there's a lot of real-estate activity in this section and that means business for us."

"Us? You have a partner?"

"You'll meet him." She nodded without looking at me. "I found somebody."

"That's the best news, Chottie."

She nodded again. "Yes. I did the other, though. What I was afraid I'd do, out of loneliness and desperation. He wasn't a gigolo with patent-leather hair. He was a young writer, very unsuccessful *and*, I found out, not very talented. I had a hard time getting rid of him."

"How did you?"

"I gave him money to go to Mexico."

"That doesn't always work."

"Not if you have no one else, but now I have someone else."

"Tell me about him."

"Oh, I will. He's married, of course. Separated from his wife. He's fifty, has two grown children that live with her, down in Whittier. That's on the other side of Los Angeles. He's a landscape architect and that's how I met him."

"And what of the future?"

"His wife won't give him a divorce till the daughter gets married, but that will be in June, when she finishes college. Then we have over a year to wait, but what's a year? The wife is as anxious to get out of it as he is, but not before the girl is married off. He has a room over in

Santa Monica. Most of his work is around here. Brentwood Heights. Beverly. Bel-Air. He isn't really my partner yet, but I don't know what I'd do without him. I
couldn't."

We had a good dinner, starting, as Californians do,
with a salad, and we talked without pause until nine-
thirty,when the doorbell rang. "That's Lou. On the dot.
By the way, he knows about you and our one matinée,
so don't mind if he sizes you up."

Louis Grafmiller was a stocky, sunburned man with
close-cropped iron-gray hair. "Hello, Catherine," he said,
and kissed her on the lips. He shook hands with me
and it was a firm handshake.

"Glad to know you, Mr. Malloy," he said. "This girl is
always singing your praises."

"Well, she's just finished singing some of yours," I
said.

"Have a drink, Lou?"

"Oh, a glass of wine, maybe. Some of that Chianti?
You just get in from the East?"

"Monday."

"Your first visit to California, Catherine said."

"Yes, I'd never been west of the Mississippi before."

"It's a big country, and a good country. People don't
realize how big or how good. They ought to get around
more and see what they have before they turn it over
to the Communists. I know I didn't vote to take it away
from Wall Street just to hand it over to those other
bastards."

I had a quick revelation of what he would do to Chottie's gigolo writer if he ever showed up again. She was well protected now.

"I understand your book is a big success. Do you know Ernest Hemingway?"

"No."

"I like his kind of writing. Catherine gave me your book but I haven't started it yet."

"Are you going to write another, Jim?" said Chottie.

"Yes, when I go back. I don't think I'll stay out here past the first option."

"Don't you like California?" he smiled.

"Not yet. I don't dislike it yet, either. But I'll never be a Californian."

"That's what I said twenty-five years ago, but I'm still here. There are only two states that have everything. California, and Pennsylvania."

"I'm from Pennsylvania."

"I know. So am I. Pittsburgh. You're from the other end of the state. I have cousins in Reading."

Now slowly I was conscious of Chottie's changed face as she listened to our conversation; it was very right that her face should be different when she herself was so different as well. Her face, her name, and the domesticity were all new to me. I was still very fond of what I could remember, but when I left her house she shook hands with me, did not kiss me, and we were both reconciled to the finality of the farewell. Grafmiller walked with me to my car and gave me directions for

getting back to Hollywood, and I could not help thinking that he had likewise directed Chottie, but not in the
way I was headed. We did not bother to shake hands.
Neither of us regarded the introduction as a true meeting, and we paid this silent respect to our harmless
mutual animosity.

I never heard from her after that night, although I
often went to Hollywood to work on movie scripts.
Once on an impulse I looked up Grafmiller in the
telephone book and his address was the same as the
house where I had met him, hers. Then I heard some-
where that he had died, but the information came long
after his death and I did not write to Chottie. She was
swallowed up in the anonymity of former movie stars
living in Los Angeles—the easiest way for a former
movie star to become obscure—until Joe Finston put
her in *Benediction at Dawn*. In today's obituaries there
is mention of Louis Grafmiller, but not a word about
their greenhouse, and for some reason or other that
pleased me. On the same page there was an obituary
of a man who had once won the 500 mile race at Indian-
apolis but who died while playing shuffleboard at St.
Petersburg, Florida.

I close this reminiscence with one more fact. Thomas
Rodney Hunterden was born Thomas Robert Hunt-
zinger in Gibbsville, Pa. I have no idea why he disliked
my father, and I am long past caring.